Death of a Showgirl

Tobias Jones is the author of three works of non-fiction and two novels.

He has written and presented documentaries for the BBC and for RAI, the Italian state broadcaster, and has been a columnist for both the *Observer* and *Internazionale*.

He's the co-founder and Warden of Windsor Hill Wood, a shelter for people undergoing a period of crisis in their lives.

www.tobias-jones.com
www.windsorhillwood.co.uk

Death of a Showgirl

Tobias Jones

faber and faber

First published in this edition in 2013
by Faber and Faber Limited
Bloomsbury House
74–77 Great Russell Street
London WC1B 3DA

Typeset by Faber and Faber Ltd
Printed and bound by CPI Group (UK) Ltd, Croydon, CR0 4YY

A CIP record for this book
is available from the British Library

ISBN 978-0-571-26969-3

2 4 6 8 10 9 7 5 3 1

For David and Vandana

It was almost ten at night when I finally found Fausto Biondi's villa. A couple of cars honked loudly as I slowed down to manoeuvre my wheels onto the pavement. It had taken over five hours to get here and my limbs were stiff as I opened the car door and swung out my legs. I rotated my gammy ankle and looked up at the imposing palazzo. Most of it was obscured by a large solid metal gate. I got out, walked to the intercom and pushed in the transparent rectangle.

A gruff male voice came on immediately. 'Who is it?'

'Castagnetti.'

'About time.' The line went dead and the gate swung open to reveal a mansion that looked like a doll's house: perfectly symmetrical with five large windows on each floor. I got back in the car and drove in. Lights flicked on as the car hit automatic sensors, flooding the white gravel drive in a chill light.

A man was standing in the doorway as I got out.

'What's taken you so long?' he scowled.

'I had to do my make-up.'

He looked at my unshaven face without smiling. He was a tall man with a strong face and grey hair. Probably late fifties, I thought. He had half-moon glasses resting on his chest, their arms attached to a cord that went around his neck.

'Fausto Biondi.' He held out a hand. We shook and he led me

inside. The place was eerily clean and our footsteps echoed on the marble as he led me into a reception room. An entire wall was lined with the tan leather spines of antiquarian books. On another wall were ancient oil paintings, hung close together so that the effect was dark and sombre. On one of the three sofas was a thin, tense woman who was holding a glass in both hands as if she were nervously praying.

'Good evening,' she said weakly, putting her glass down and trying to push herself up off the sofa.

'My wife, Giovanna.' Biondi nodded his head in her direction. Then he pointed at me. 'This is the detective, Castagnetti.'

She was still trying to stand up but wobbled badly. Her husband caught her and took the glass out of her hand.

'You're drinking too much,' he hissed.

She ignored him and turned to me, offering a limp paw, fingers down, as if she expected me to kiss it rather than shake it. I did what I could with those cold fingers, holding them as she looked at me with imploring eyes. Her face was puffy and pasty, framed by hair that looked unbrushed.

'It's a pleasure,' she said with the sort of deliberation that suggested she was concentrating on not slurring her words.

'You said on the phone . . .' I began, hoping one of them would pick up the story.

'Please.' Biondi motioned with his hand to one of the sofas. 'Sit down.'

I sa

nk back into the cushions and the two of them stood there awkwardly, side by side but decidedly distant.

'Our daughter is missing,' he said bluntly.

I nodded. 'What's she called?'

'Simona.'

'Any nicknames?'

'Just Simona,' he said impatiently.

'And how long has she been missing?'

'Since yesterday morning. She went out to do some shopping and never came back. We waited for her at lunch and she didn't come home. Her phone was switched off. Still is. She never switches off her phone. She's on it all the time. Always sending messages to her friends. Bloody beep-beep every two minutes.'

'And you've informed the authorities?'

'Called them last night. They're useless. They ask a couple of questions and then clear off. They say she's an adult and probably just wants an adventure. They said there's no evidence of any crime having been committed.'

At the mention of the word 'crime' the wife gave an involuntary yelp. Biondi looked at her like she was an irritation and turned back to me.

'We haven't slept all night.' He looked at his wife as if it were her fault. 'I'm afraid we're very tense.'

'She's an adult, you said. How old is she?'

'Only just eighteen,' the wife said. She was shaking badly and muttering something to herself.

'And what was she wearing?'

'Jeans. T-shirt. The same as every other teenager,' Biondi said.

'Colour?'

'Of the T-shirt? It was red.'

'OK,' I took it in slowly, trying to weigh up the probability

3

that the girl had gone absent voluntarily from this tense household.

'Does Simona have a boyfriend?'

'No,' he said brusquely.

'Is she,' I hesitated, 'sexually active?'

'You make her sound like an animal.'

'I've got other phrases if you prefer.'

He scowled at me and I held his stare. I was getting tired of the spiteful atmosphere. We stared at each other for another second and he eventually dropped his chin on his chest, looking over at his wife from the corner of his eye. 'Is she?' he asked.

'I don't know. She hasn't ever said anything to me. She's never even had a boyfriend. Not a real boyfriend.'

'And you've no idea why she would run away?'

'She hasn't run away,' he said aggressively. 'Something's happened to her.'

I nodded, not wanting to say anything else that might antagonise him. As we stood there I could hear footsteps in the hall, quick clicks on the marble floor that sounded urgent. A tall, elegant woman came into the room with a tray of sandwiches.

'Hello,' she said to me as she put the tray on the long low table in front of the sofa.

'This is our elder daughter,' Biondi said. 'Chiara.'

We nodded at each other and shook hands. She must have been much older than Simona, in her mid or late thirties. Almost my age, I thought, without knowing why. She looked young enough to be reckless, but old enough to get away with it. She had an hourglass figure and her yellow dress didn't leave much to the imagination.

'Have you got a photograph?' I asked.

4

'I'll get it,' Chiara said, as if there were only one in the whole household. Her heels sounded like the crack of a whip as she paced off. I watched her as she went: the back of her dress was almost down to the small of her back, revealing warm, tanned skin.

'Prego,' Biondi said to me, motioning towards the sandwiches. It was almost his first act of courtesy. I took one and then another. I hadn't eaten since starting the drive south soon after lunch.

'Drink?'

'Just water.'

He moved over to a drinks trolley and I saw him put a glass stopper back on a bottle of clear liquid. He poured two glasses of water and then gave them to me and his wife. We stood there like that, waiting for Chiara to come back. Biondi was frowning at everything he laid eyes on.

She came back and stood beside me so that our upper arms were touching. She was holding a magazine that looked thin. She passed it over to me and the paper felt as flimsy as aluminium foil. I shut it to look at the cover. *Moda*, it was called. It was one of the standard gossip mags full of photos and fashion and guesses about what the stars were wearing or who they were seeing. I turned back to the page Chiara had shown me and looked at a collage of snaps, all printed as if they were Polaroids. There were captions written in the white space below.

'That's her,' Chiara said, pointing out a young girl with a broad smile. The caption said 'Simona Biondi at Oro Nightclub'. Simona was pulling the sort of sideways impish pose – cheekbone on shoulder – that people sometimes adopt when they're being snapped. She looked coy and coquettish, with big dark eyes and a smile that seemed genuinely carefree. She certainly looked like Chiara: the sisters both had the same bee-stung lips. The whole page showed similar shots: one-off pictures of beautiful people at fashionable clubs.

'You mind if I keep this?' I asked.

'Prego.' She shrugged. 'Simona bought a dozen anyway. She thought it was the beginning of her career.'

'I told her,' the father growled, 'that you can't make a career out of being snapped in nightclubs but she wouldn't listen.'

'Did she go out a lot?'

'She's just a little girl,' the mother said in her frail voice.

'Once a week, like all teenagers,' the sister said. 'She went out on a Saturday night with friends, that was it.' She had a husky sort of voice, the kind of voice that always sounded like a come-on.

'Would you mind showing me her bedroom?'

The father moved, but Chiara stopped him. 'I'll go.'

I followed her out of the room, back towards the front door. On the right was a staircase so wide that a dozen people could walk up side by side. Each time the staircase turned a corner there was a large statue or sculpture. The whole place oozed money but no warmth.

'What line's your father in?' I asked idly as we got to the landing at the top.

She stopped to look at me as if I were being critical. 'He's a lawyer.'

We walked to the end of the corridor and into a large bedroom.

'This is the room,' she said, like an estate agent showing me round.

I walked in and looked at the scene. There was a wall of walnut wood that I assumed was a wardrobe. Magazines and books were everywhere. There were a couple of chargers on the bed. There was a door off to the left, and I wandered in: an ensuite bathroom containing enough bottles to wash a car. I opened the wooden doors and saw metres of clothes. A central column of shelves must have held more than two dozen pairs of shoes. No money worries here, I thought. The sister was automatically tidying up, closing books and putting them on shelves.

'Leave it,' I said. 'Leave it as it is.'

'Of course,' she said, straightening up. 'Sorry.'

I opened a few drawers. There were no surprises. Just clothing, a lot of clothing, and more magazines. No pills, condoms, letters.

'Can you tell me a bit more about your sister?' I asked.

Chiara was over by the window with her back to me and I saw her shoulders bouncing like she was silently sneezing. I moved to the side and saw that she had one hand over her mouth. I watched her for a minute, her body juddering as she cried. Eventually she gave up trying to be silent and wept openly. She looked more openly distraught about the disappearance than either of her parents, and yet at the same time more rational, more together than either of them. Her father seemed to think it was an affront to him that Simona had gone missing; Chiara seemed only concerned that Simona might be in danger.

'I'm sorry,' she said once she had pulled herself together.

She went back to looking out of the window and started speaking as if in a trance. 'Simona is just a lovely girl. She's a very smart, kind girl.'

'Has anything happened recently that might have made her want to leave home?'

She shook her head. 'She's been retreating into herself for a year or two now. She's become obsessed about her own privacy and space. This is the first time I've been in this room for months. But that's normal. All teenagers want that. They all want their own room to be a haven from parental interference. They need to establish themselves in their own world. Simona was doing that, pushing them away a bit, but that's normal. It's very normal.'

'And she gets on OK with your parents?'

She shrugged. 'Our parents aren't exactly easy to live with.'

'Why not?'

'You've seen them. My father has the civility of a goose. He's got a short fuse and a long memory. Won't forget any wrong that's ever been done to him. And my mother is a nervous wreck. Always has been, even before Simona went missing. I can't imagine how Simona survives here on her own with the two of them.'

'You don't live here?'

'No. God no. I've got my own family. I left home a couple of years after Simona was born, so it's like she's grown up as an only child. At least when I was growing up my father had some graces left. And Mother was working back then, so I hardly saw her.'

'What does she do?'

'She doesn't any more. She was a doctor. She was always at work when I was growing up. I spent more time with a nanny than I ever did with her. But then she had some sort of breakdown and never went back to work. She started self-medicating, taking all sorts of pills and washing them down with anything she could find on the drinks trolley. It's kind of funny. I used to be jealous of Simona growing up with Mother in the house, because I never had that. I never really spent much time with my own mother. But I think I actually had it a whole lot easier. Simona's grown up with this weepy, self-pitying wreck who just lies around and expects to be waited on.' She stopped herself. 'I'm sorry, but that's how it is.'

'And Simona waits on her?'

'She's an angel, an absolute angel. She's been my mother's nurse for years. I mean, they've got a woman who does the shopping and cooking and the like, but Simona's the one who does the emotional chores.'

'Like what?'

'Listening to Mother when she gets weepy, soothing my father when he's irate. It's like she's the parent and they're the stroppy children.'

'You don't think she just got bored of being a nurse? Wanted a break?'

'I'm sure she did. I know she did. We've talked about it. I tried to persuade her to come and live with us a while back.'

'And?'

'She said she would have loved to. Her eyes lit up at the idea. She loves my children, absolutely adores them. But she said she couldn't leave Mother on her own like that.' Chiara stared at me to make sure I was listening. 'That's why she wouldn't just disappear like this. She wouldn't dream of abandoning Mother, of causing them all this pain. She's so thoughtful. It's just not possible.'

'But she wanted to leave?'

She sighed noisily, almost as if she were growling at my questions. 'She's eighteen. Everyone that age wants to start living their own life. And she was growing resentful, secretly I mean. She never let on, but I'm sure she was wise enough to know that she was being exploited by childish parents. She was restless. She did want to find her own space, live her own life.'

'Isn't that what she's doing now?'

'No!' she shouted. 'No.' She stared at me with her fiery eyes. 'I've told you, she wouldn't put us through this.' She dropped her head as if someone had cut the puppet's strings. 'All I'm saying is that she was uncomfortable here. It's a cold, loveless house. She didn't feel at home here any more. She didn't feel close to my parents, didn't have any sort of bond with them other than that of the nurse for the patient. That's no basis for a mutual adult relationship.'

'I understand.'

She stared at the bed in silence and I studied her face. She looked like a proud, defiant woman. There was something very enticing about her. She had high cheekbones, thick lips and large eyes. But there was more than a hint of sorrow in her face, as if she had survived traumas in the past and expected them in the future.

She must have felt my gaze because she suddenly looked up at me. 'And this is what you do, is it?'

'What?'

'You're a private detective?'

I moved my head from side to side like I wasn't sure. 'I don't normally call myself that.'

'Why not?'

'Because then people expect me to carry a magnifying glass or wear a trilby.'

'But that's your job?'

'Sure.'

She looked me up and down as though it were a job interview. 'You look very young.'

'I feel old on the inside.'

'Me too,' she said. We both looked at each other like we had a bond. In another situation I would have pulled her towards me, but this wasn't the time or place. She looked at the floor and then back at me with imploring eyes. There was something warm but off-hand about her, I thought: an unusual combination that suggested she was self-contained but wished she wasn't. I guessed she was probably in an unhappy marriage. But then that's a percentage assumption about most people.

'What are the chances?' she said.

'Of what?'

'Finding her safe and well?'

I must have hesitated because her face dropped. She closed her eyes as if I were already breaking bad news.

'It's very likely I'll find her,' I said slowly.

'Alive?'

'I can't say that. I hope so. It's perfectly probable she'll come home unharmed.'

She sighed again, less noisily this time.

'Where's this Oro?' I asked.

'What?'

'The nightclub where that photo was taken?'

'It's in Testaccio.'

'I should get round there.'

We walked down the staircase. I saw her running her hands along the wide flat bannisters as if searching for support.

'Allora?' shouted Biondi before we were even at the bottom. 'Did you find anything?'

'Of course we didn't,' the sister interrupted.

'Then why did you go up there?'

'Please, Father.' She slammed a hand on the circle of wood at the end of the bannister. 'Try and be civil. He's trying to build up a picture of who he's looking for.'

Biondi stared at me like he was already disappointed. 'Va bene, va bene,' he said, though he didn't sound convinced. 'Come into my study and we'll sort out your fee.'

I nodded at Chiara by way of goodbye and followed Biondi into a room at the end of the house. There were more untouched tomes in here and a large desk with a green leather inlay. The room's rug looked like an heirloom from the Middle Ages.

'How much?'

I told him my daily rate and he pulled out a drawer and counted some notes.

'I'll need expenses as well.'

'Of course you will,' he said sarcastically.

If I hadn't been concerned about the fate of a young girl, I would have walked out there and then. I was tired of his rudeness and discourtesy but I bit my tongue and said nothing. He was the kind of man who got his own way but no pleasure from it. His face at rest was a scowl, and when animated was a grimace. He seemed to hold a grudge against the world. He was abrupt and discourteous, but very openly so, and I wondered if there was an honesty there, if maybe Biondi's causticity wasn't preferable to the mellifluous deceit I had seen so many times before. It was the wrong time to judge him anyway. He looked like the type who was always highly strung, and – with his daughter missing – he seemed about to snap.

I thanked him as he passed me a thin wad of notes.

'Please find her. Bring her home.'

'I'll do everything I can.'

He stood up and we shook hands. He took mine in both of his, a rare show of solidarity or encouragement. 'Please . . .' he said beseechingly.

As we walked back into the large reception room the frail wife came stumbling towards us. 'I'm going to try and get some sleep,' she said. 'Good night.' She offered me her fingers again. I clasped them and gave a slight deferential bow.

Biondi walked me towards the front door repeating his wife's phrase: '"Going to try and get some sleep" . . . the amount of pills she takes, it's a wonder she ever wakes up.'

'What does she take them for?'

'The pills? To sleep, to wake up, to get out of bed, to digest, to regress. There's hardly any activity that isn't accompanied by some pill being knocked back.'

'It must be a very trying time.' It sounded condescending or false and he nodded brusquely.

'Buonanotte,' he said, reaching to his right to open the monumental gate that kept the swarming city at bay.

I got back in the car and looked up at the sad house once more. I saw the mother, Giovanna, silhouetted in an upstairs window. The window looked twice her height as she drew the curtains. The car crunched on the gravel and the gate closed behind me as I waited for a space to enter the busy Saturday night traffic.

The three-lane road ran parallel to the Tiber. Motorbikes kept roaring past me, weaving between the traffic as the tyres swayed out flamboyantly from under the drivers. It was a warm night and most cars had their windows down. Each time we stopped at traffic lights I heard their thumping music and felt the vibrations through my seat. It was as if each car was competing with the next to impose their beat. Men were leaning out of windows trying to make the girls in other cars laugh. Someone on a moped recognised a friend on another moped and they bumped gloved knuckles like boxers before a bout.

It was a long time since I had been in Rome. I had forgotten the energy and noise of the place. It seemed to come alive at night like the throbbing, insistent sound of cicadas after sunset. I sped past ancient floodlit monuments, past the august cupolas and famous ruins. Immaculate shop displays were illuminated and there were small crowds even now, nocturnal window shopping under the palm trees.

I tried to remember which bridge I needed to cross to get to Testaccio. I overshot and had to turn round and go back up the river the other way: more traffic lights, more loud music, more banter.

There was a procession of drivers looking for somewhere to park. Most of the cars around here seemed abandoned rather

14

than parked. They had just put a wheel or two on the pavement and left it at that. I went up and down narrow cobbled streets and eventually found a small patch of pavement I could claim as my own. I ripped the snap of Simona out of the magazine and twisted my body sideways to get out of the car.

There was a bar on the corner of the street. It was one of those expensive, sedate places where the waiters wore uniforms. I sat down and ordered a coffee. The guy came back with a small steaming thimble and the scontrino.

'You know where the Oro nightclub is?' I asked as I passed him some coins.

'Sure,' he said, nodding cheerfully like he wished he was there. He gave me directions and then looked at me with his head cocked to one side. 'With respect, you don't look like the usual Oro punter.'

I ran my hand across my short greying hair and looked at my clothes. I was wearing an old pair of trousers and a shirt that had seen better days. 'Underdressed?' I asked.

'Underdressed and overage,' he smiled.

'It's a young crowd in there?'

He nodded. 'Young and pretty wild.'

I told him I was looking for my daughter. I showed him the photo of Simona and he took it and held it towards the old-fashioned lantern advertising a beer brand that was hanging from a corner of the awning. He shook his head and wished me luck.

I picked up the sachet from the saucer, ripped off the corner and poured in some sugar. I stirred and knocked back the scalding rich liquid. There were young kids playing on the steps of a monument in the middle of the small square. Behind them were the pillars and pediment of an ancient church.

The man's directions led me towards a main road on the other side of the suburb's narrow streets. There were a few dolled-up kids waiting to cross the road with me and I followed them to what looked like an abandoned industrial complex sandwiched in the fork between two roads.

The name of the place, Oro, was written in illuminated golden letters. I could hear the thumping music reverberating outside. There must have been about a hundred people in the queue, all chattering away. The men looked like they were dressed for a day's work in the bank: white shirts, stiff collars, smart shoes, immaculately combed hair. The women were more exotic. Under their jackets, most of them seemed to be wearing more make-up than clothing.

I took out the snap of Simona and started walking up and down the queue, asking if anyone had seen her. One man joked that he wouldn't mind getting to know her and his friends guffawed. Another, a young girl with glitter on her powdered cheeks, said that she looked familiar. No one said anything useful. I joined the back of the queue.

It took almost an hour to get in. Two bouncers with transparent plastic earpieces and microphones on the lapels of their jackets clearly enjoyed their power. They unhooked a thick red rope occasionally to let a couple of people in and then hooked it back up for another ten minutes, ignoring the impatient punters. Both had shaved heads like blond sandpaper.

When I finally got to the front of the queue the two men looked at me with obvious disdain.

'You sure you're in the right place?' one of them asked.

'This is Oro, right?'

He nodded as if it were obvious. The back of his neck created rolls like thick sausages as he rocked his head back and forth.

'Then I'm in the right place.'

'Right place, wrong clothes,' he said. 'We can't let you in dressed like that.'

I reached into my back pocket and pulled out my badge. It was a licence to practise as a private detective. I put a couple of Biondi's notes underneath it and passed it over.

'I'm looking for a girl,' I said as he pocketed the notes and passed back the badge.

'Aren't we all?' He smiled.

'Have you seen this one? She's called Simona.'

He took the snap out of my hand and shook his head.

'You?' I said to his uninterested colleague. He reached over, took the snap, and passed it back. He clicked his tongue and put his head to one side as he lifted the twisted red rope and let me in.

As soon as I went through the double doors the temperature and volume soared. People were checking in their coats and their modesty in a booth to the right. As I went through the next set of doors the music became deafening. I could feel it booming inside my ribcage as I watched random limbs illuminated by strobe lighting. Most of the dancers had their hands in the air and all those arms looked like waving underwater seaweed.

The girls were dressed for the beach: bikinis with mini sarongs wrapped round their waists. Some had exotic headgear on: feathers or sombreros. One or two of the men had taken their tops off and everywhere I looked I could see skin dripping with oil or sweat. There were vertical poles on plinths where various women were cavorting, wrapping their thighs around the golden metal and grinding to the music.

I tried to ask a couple of people if they recognised the photograph but no one could hear what I was saying. I showed it to one girl who put her hands straight in the air and danced around me until her elbows were on my shoulders. She moved her arms backwards and forwards so that her bosom bounced against my midriff. I stood there motionless as she started to move up and down me. She shouted something in my ear but I couldn't understand what she was saying. She turned round, dancing away from me while looking over her shoulder. The few people managing to make conversation were having to shout into each other's ears so that they almost ended up embracing, touching each other's bodies to balance themselves.

There was a slightly quieter side-room behind the pulsating dance floor where people were lounging around on sofas. Behind them a scratchy film of some urban underpass was being projected onto the wall. There was a couple making out on an armchair, their hands exploring each other's bodies. Everyone seemed to be holding small plastic bottles of water.

I sat down on a bar stool and watched the strange film being projected onto the opposite wall. The underpass was in shade, but the light beyond it was so bright that the edges of the overhead road were blurred, like the camera was deliberately overexposing. I guessed it was LA or somewhere in California. Nothing much happened. Occasionally some rubbish was thrown from above, or an animal wandered into view trying to find food amongst the detritus. It seemed pointless, but maybe that was the point.

'May I?' a voice said to my right.

I looked over and a young girl was standing there asking if she could sit next to me. I gestured to say 'no problem'.

'This looks interesting,' she said.

I wasn't sure if she was serious. I turned to look at her. She was beautiful. Probably still a teenager. As undressed as everyone else. Her skin was dark, but I could just see the tan lines on her breasts which, judging by the way she was leaning forward, was what I was supposed to see.

'I'm Sara,' she said.

'Casta.'

'Who are you with?'

'No one.'

'You're on your own?' She seemed incredulous.

I nodded. 'I'm looking for a girl.'

She misunderstood, seeming to think I was there just for a crude pick-up, and looked disconcerted. So I showed her the snap.

'Who's that?' She read the caption. 'Simona Biondi. Who's she?'

'She's gone missing. She was in here a week or two ago when this was taken.'

'Never seen her. Sorry. She your daughter?'

'Do I look that old?'

She looked me over. 'Who is she?'

'Just a girl,' I said.

She sat next to me for a while and we watched the weird film.

Eventually she stood up and announced she was going to have a dance. I told her I would see her around.

The bar was three deep and the only way to get served was to waft a note in the air. People at the front retreated from the bar with bottles held above their heads. I was pushed forward by impatient punters.

After an uncomfortable quarter of an hour, the sweating barman offered me his ear, hoping to hear my order.

'Have you seen her?' I shouted, pointing down at the photo and showing him my badge.

He looked down at it and then at me. He pulled himself up onto the bar, resting his stomach on the wet chrome surface to yell something in my ear. I shook my head to tell him I hadn't heard. He tried again, but all I got were strange sounds and some spit.

He jumped back down to the floor and beckoned me towards the end of the bar. He gestured to his white-shirted colleagues that he was heading off for two minutes and then lifted up a hinged section of the bar, shooing people off it. He nodded with his head, telling me to come in. He ignored the wall of arms holding notes towards him between the taps and led me up some stairs behind the bar.

'Cazzo,' he said, turning round to wait for me at the top of the steps. 'I'll be deaf by the time I'm thirty if I stay working here.'

He led me into a small office with a large window overlooking the dance floor. 'What is it with this girl?' he said, turning to face me. He was a young, good-looking lad with dark curls as if a haircut was a month or two overdue.

'How do you mean?' I said, intrigued.

'Just the other day I had an old man coming round here with that same photo, asking exactly the same question.'

'Asking what exactly?'

'If I had seen the girl.'

'And had you?'

He shrugged. 'I serve hundreds of people every night. Probably a few thousand a week. Chances are I've served her if she's been in here.'

The boy had a southern accent. Somewhere from Puglia, I guessed.

'And what did you tell the man?'

'Exactly that. That I had probably served her.' He shrugged again impatiently, as if there was nothing more to say.

'And what did he say to that?'

'He offered me two hundred to call him if she ever came in again. Left me a copy of that photo and a number to call him on.'

'You still got that number?'

'Sure. If it was worth two hundred, I wasn't going to lose it.'

I raised my chin to tell him to get it. He stood up and went over to a wall of jackets and bags. He found his own and unzipped an inside pocket. He showed me the copy of the magazine snap and passed me a piece of paper: *Massimo Mori* was written in biro, with, underneath, *Hotel del Fiume. Room 13*. There was a mobile number below that.

'Hotel del Fiume? Where's that?' I asked, holding up the paper.

'Boh,' he said, throwing his thumbs out sideways to say he didn't know. 'He just told me to call him on that number if I ever saw her. I didn't see her so I didn't call him.'

'Massimo Mori, eh? That's his name?'

'That's what he said. I didn't think any more about it until you came in.' He looked at me with curiosity. 'What's all this about.'

'Describe the man, this Mori,' I said, ignoring his question.

He stared vacantly at the wall. 'He looked a bit like an ageing rocker. You know, he must have been middle-aged or more but he had his grey hair in a ponytail. We occasionally get types like that in here: the older crowd who come in looking to pick up a girl.'

'Doesn't seem very hard to do around here.'

'No.' He chuckled, his gaze losing focus as he smiled.

I looked through the window and onto the dance floor. Down below there were two girls dancing with their wrists together above their heads, moving them left and right with their eyes closed. Each had a bare thigh between the other's legs. I watched them as they started kissing, a circle of spectators egging them on.

'He was short, I remember that much. Short with a grey ponytail. That's about it.'

'Did he say why he was looking for the girl?'

'He said,' he looked at me through his eyebrows as if he weren't sure, 'that she was his daughter. We get that in here. Some sad father who is looking for a wayward child.'

'Or a wayward wife?'

'And that.' He chuckled again. 'I didn't buy it. I mean, he looked dodgy to me. There was something about him I didn't trust.'

'Why not?'

'I get to see a whole lot of faces every night. You get quite

22

good at judging them after a while. You know what they're like somehow. And he looked dodgy, that's all. To be honest, I'm not certain I would have called him even if she had turned up. I mean, sure, I need the money, but he wasn't her father. Even I knew that. He had the wrong face, the wrong attitude.'

'What about my face?' I asked. 'Would you call me if she came in again?'

He looked at me and narrowed his eyes. 'You look like a tough nut. But that limp you've got makes you seem like you've been through it.' He was serious now, like he might have been through it, whatever it was, himself. 'Why do you want her?'

'Because she's gone missing. She didn't come home last night. I'm a private detective hired by her parents to bring her home.' I showed him my badge.

'So that guy wasn't her father?'

I shook my head.

'Didn't think so.' He looked suddenly sheepish. 'I sure could have done with that money though.'

I reached into my pocket a passed him a note. 'I'll keep this card,' I said, holding up the business card from the Hotel del Fiume. 'If you see this Massimo Mori, or the girl again, call me immediately and I'll give you that two hundred.' I ripped a page out of my notebook and wrote my number on it. 'There's no CCTV here?'

He shook his head. 'I don't think the owners would want that.'

'Why not?'

He looked around the small office, just to double-check no one else was around. 'It's better that what goes on in here doesn't get recorded for posterity.'

'How do you mean?'

He didn't reply, but gestured towards the window. I looked down again at the crowded floor beneath. The hedonism was explicit and, I guessed, much of it wasn't legal.

'I better get back,' he said.

I followed him down the stairs and into the bar. There were even more people waving notes now, all looking desperate and needy. He snapped the top off a beer bottle and passed it to me. Then he reopened the hinged bit of the bar and let me back out into the melee. I sank the beer and walked out. It was well past midnight now and the air was unexpectedly cool. There were people in groups of twos and threes smoking spliffs and cigarettes, trying to adjust to the reality of the outside world.

I walked slowly back to my car, wondering about the Oro club and why a girl like Simona would come here. It was a heady sort of place, the kind of place that could knock you off balance if you didn't have your feet on the ground. I yanked the car off the pavement and drove back through the cobbled alleyways onto the main road.

The street cleaners were at work now, taking advantage of the almost empty roads to clear up the day's droppings. The circular brushes underneath their little vehicles looked like the whirling discs of an electric toothbrush as they angled down into the plaque between the road and the pavement. Binmen in bright hi-vis vests were jovially shouting to each other from one side of the road to the other.

There were still quite a few late-night revellers standing around outside bars or at traffic lights. Older couples were walking serenely through the city as though it were the middle of the day. I looked at the clock on the dashboard and saw it was just gone two.

I pulled up by one of the binmen and showed him the hotel's business card.

'Hotel del Fiume?' He frowned and shook his head. 'Hang on.' He called over a colleague and a long conference ensued about where it might be. They thought it was in opposite parts of the city and argued cheerfully for a few minutes.

'Why don't you just call them and ask?' one of them said when they couldn't come to an agreement.

'All I've got is the name of the place,' I said.

'You're not likely to get a bed then, are you?'

'Not looking for a bed. I'm trying to find a girl.'

They looked at me with sympathy, as though I were some sort of sad cuckold. I showed them the snap just in case, but of course they just shrugged and moved away like they didn't want to get involved.

I drove on and found a taxi rank with no taxis but a lot of punters queueing up to get home. I parked and walked up and down the queue, asking if anyone knew where the hotel was. Most of them tried to help, offering their vague ideas. When a taxi eventually rolled up the couple getting in let me ask the driver, and he seemed convinced it was over towards Ostia. Since that seemed to be the consensus, I got back in the car and headed towards the sea.

As I left the city behind me I became aware of the darkness. No more street lights, no more glitzy shop windows. Just a few silhouettes of cypresses against the moonlight. I was overcome by tiredness. I had been driving almost all day and now all I needed was a bed.

It wasn't long before I got to Ostia, the seaside suburb of Rome. The air smelt different here: salty with hints of seaweed and the accumulated smells of a resort on a Saturday night: bonfires, caramelised nuts, spilt drinks. I drove as far as the Lido, knowing I had arrived when I saw the sand on the pavements. The whole place was almost entirely abandoned now. There was just one couple walking along the beach, looking like they were in the middle of an argument. The man kept grabbing the woman as she walked away. She twisted out of his grasp, but was too drunk or desperate to make a clean break, and always seemed to let him take hold of her again.

There were two dozen shallow street signs hanging off one post and I saw, half-way down, the name of the hotel. I turned right and followed the signs through dull, dark streets. When I got to the hotel the vertical sign with its one star wasn't even illuminated. I got out and shut the door quietly. If Massimo Mori was here with the girl I didn't want him awake.

The door to the place was locked. Amongst the colourful stickers listing the credit cards they accepted and the associations they belonged to was a handwritten card saying *If Closed, Ring Bell.* The arrow pointed to a small buzzer. I held it down for a few seconds. Nothing.

Stepping back, I couldn't see any lights on. I walked around the corner to see the place from the other street but it was all dark. Most of the curtains in the rooms weren't drawn so I guessed they had hardly any guests.

I rang the buzzer again, holding it down for ten, fifteen seconds. I took my finger off and then went again. So much for the element of surprise.

From inside I heard a man cursing. He seemed to be kicking furniture on his way to the door. When he got closer I could see that he was short and fat, with a short-sleeved shirt thrown over a dirty white vest. He unlocked the door and stared at me.

'What the fuck do you want?'

'You always receive your guests like that?'

He screwed his face up. He looked like a bulldog. He was old and unshaven and smelt of booze. His hair was thin and sparse, though. No grey ponytail.

'I'm looking for a bed for the night,' I said.

'Look elsewhere.' He started shutting the door. I gave it a good shove with my shoulder and he stumbled sideways, putting out a hand to break his fall. I closed the door behind me and started pulling him roughly to his feet.

'Try to be polite,' I said. 'I've had a long day.'

'Fuck you,' he said.

I let him go again and he fell back to the floor. He was half-asleep and half-drunk and it wasn't much of a fight. He rolled onto his side to try to push himself up but kept looking over his shoulder to see where I was.

'Get up,' I said impatiently.

He was swearing and grunting under his breath as he got to his feet. He didn't say anything but just stared at me with snarling contempt.

'This is the Hotel del Fiume, right?'

He smiled sarcastically, like I was really clever.

'You've got a guest here called Massimo Mori.'

He shook his head.

'You haven't got a guest here called Massimo Mori?'

He shook his head again, raising his wiry eyebrows slightly to show his enjoyment at being uncooperative.

I looked around the place with disdain. 'You got any guests in this shit-hole?'

He just stared at me. I don't know if it was exhaustion or concern for Simona, but I felt the furies rising up inside me. Suddenly I found myself lunging towards him. I got my grip around the front of his thick stubbly neck and I pushed him up against the wall.

'A young girl has been abducted,' I whispered loudly into his ear. 'From what I've been told, the man who abducted her was staying in this pit.' I gave the neck a squeeze and jammed his head back against the wall.

I let him go and he fell forward, coughing and holding his

throat. I took out some notes and held them in front of him. His gaze followed them like I was a hypnotist.

'Massimo Mori. Is he here?'

He shook his head, just like before. I was about to lunge again but he started explaining. 'We had a guest here called Mori. He checked out this morning.'

'Show me the book.'

He walked towards the thin, chest-high reception desk. He went behind it and reached down for a book. He put it on the desk and spun it round, pointing at a name. *Mori*.

'How many nights?'

'He was here for a week, more or less.' He was still rubbing his neck and looking sore.

'Was he with a girl?'

He nodded. 'Only last night.'

I pulled out the snap and put it on the desk. 'This her?'

He nodded again. 'That's the girl.'

'You sure? What was she wearing?' I asked.

'Jeans. Red T-shirt.'

I stared at him, deciding I needed him sweet. 'When did she turn up?'

'He brought her back last night.'

'Twenty-four hours ago?'

'Right. Nice piece she was. I thought he must have picked her up from the ring-road, but she was classier. You know. Didn't look like the usual hooker.'

I wasn't sure whether he was just telling me what I wanted to hear. He seemed more interested in the cash than the girl.

'What were the two of them like together? Was she being held against her will?'

'When am I going to see some of that dough? Haven't I told you enough?'

I held up the notes again. 'There. You've seen it. What were they like together?'

'What do I know what they were like together?'

I turned round to walk out. I didn't get two paces towards the door when the old boozer called me back.

'They were normal,' he shrugged grumpily. 'Just normal. A man and a woman. I see it all the time. Didn't think there was anything unusual going on.'

'He wasn't holding on to her? Wasn't mistreating her?'

'They seemed normal, OK?' He stared at me and shook his head quickly as if it might help me understand.

'When did you see them together?'

'When he brought her in last night—'

'What time?'

He shrugged. 'Ten. Eleven. And when they checked out this morning.'

'And she seemed OK?'

'To be honest, it looked like she had been crying. Didn't look exactly cheery. But then none of us do in the morning.'

'Did this Mori say where they were going?'

He shook his head impatiently. 'Allora?' He threw his chin in the air expecting his pay-off.

'What does Mori look like?'

He lowered his eyebrows, losing patience with the interrogation. 'Ugly. Long hair in a ponytail. Grey hair.' He shrugged.

'Did he have a car?'

'Sure.'

'How do you know?'

'If they want to park round here I have to give them a permit, something saying they're staying here so they can park in the blue lines.'

'So you gave him the permit?'

'Sure.'

'Did you have to write the number plate on it?'

He shook his head. 'It's just something they put on a dashboard.' He reached below the desk and showed me a plastic rectangle announcing that the owner of the vehicle was resident at the Hotel del Fiume.

'Did you see his car?'

He shook his head, staring at me as if he were pleased he couldn't help.

'But you took a photocopy of his ID?'

'Sure. That's the law.'

'Show me.'

He grunted wearily as he bent down and opened a filing cabinet. He passed over a piece of paper, a photocopy of a page of a passport. I looked at it: *Massimo Mori*, it said. The mug shot showed a man with thick eyebrows and black holes for eyes. His hair looked short.

'No ponytail here,' I said.

'Yeah, well, hair grows.'

'Not on you.'

'Have you finished?'

'Do me a copy.' I passed him back the paper. He switched on a photocopier and ran off a copy. Before handing it over, he stared at me like he deserved something in return.

'Do me a photocopy of the check-in form as well.'

He trudged back to the desk, got out another piece of paper

and ran it through the copier. I held out a twenty without looking at him. I was studying the form: it had his name and address
in black and white. The address was somewhere in Viterbo, an
hour or so to the north. Via della Salute, number 34, it said.

'I'll give you another twenty for a guided tour.'

'Forget it. I'm going to bed.'

'Fifty.'

He glared at me with his mouth open. Every feature of his
face seemed to sag. His swollen nose looked purple. He looked
to the side briefly and then back at me. 'Not much to see,' he
said.

'Show me Mori's room.'

He took a key from a hook on the wall behind him and
headed off towards the stairs. 'No lift,' he said. 'No lift so no
guests. Nowadays everyone expects a lift. And a beauty spa, and
a gym. All we've got are beds.'

'No pool?'

He snorted in derision. 'It's more like a pond. Can't afford to
clean it or heat it. It's still there, but it's a health hazard.'

The old man was puffing as he got to the first-floor landing.
He thumped a light-switch and threw his hands out like this
was all there was. There were cheap reproduction paintings on
the walls. The rug itself looked so dirty it could have been a
nature reserve.

'Which room was Mori in?'

He shuffled along the corridor and unlocked a room. There
were two double beds inside. A tiny TV was high up in the
corner, angled down towards one of the beds. The shutters
were down but as I pulled the cord to open them slightly all I

could see was a brick wall about a metre the other side of the window.

'Were both beds slept in?' I asked.

He nodded.

'How do you know? You don't clean the room yourself, do you?' He looked like the kind of person who would leave a room dirtier just for being in it.

'A girl comes in. She changed both beds this morning.'

'How do you know?'

'I asked her. I was curious about the odd couple.'

'Why odd?'

He rolled his eyes, bored of the questions. 'He was gnarled and ugly. She was young and beautiful. The only time a couple like that get together is when he's rich. This guy wasn't. So I just wondered what was going on. I asked the cleaning girl and she told me they'd used separate beds.'

I poked around the cheap furniture, pulling out drawers and opening cupboards and wardrobes. They wobbled feebly each time I pulled a handle. Their plastic laminate smelt of too much disinfectant. The bathroom was empty. There was a shower cubicle that looked half the size of a telephone kiosk. A thin miniature soap was wrapped up, ready for the next sad resident. There was a plastic bin with a translucent liner. Nothing of interest.

'What happened to the rubbish?'

'It goes in the wheelie bins in the basement. But today was rubbish day so it's already gone.'

'Nice place,' I said sarcastically.

'Wasn't always like this. Used to be a very fashionable place twenty, thirty years ago.'

'Yeah?' I said sceptically.

'Yeah. Used to have people begging to be allowed in. We used to host major conferences and gala events and parties. It used to be the perfect place for a party before they built all those new swank places right on the seafront. The parties we used to have.' He laughed at the memory. 'Incredible parties. Stuff going on you wouldn't believe. Sometimes I would walk along this corridor and I would see naked girls going from one room to the next.'

'Must have been nice for you.'

'We used to have all the stars here. You remember Alberto Grilli, the guy who presented that game show back in the eighties? He was a regular. Always tipped like a king. Great guy, Alberto. And there was Beppe Anselmi, the actor. We've got a signed photo of him downstairs.'

He went on like that, trying to persuade me that this place used to be a Mecca for stars back in the day. He led me back downstairs and showed me a gallery of framed signed photographs of people I had never heard of. He described their TV shows or films, and what they used to eat and tip and their taste in girls.

I wasn't sure if it was all just talk. Most of the bars round here have photos of stars. It seems to be standard décor. And most pizzerie have one or two pizzas named after footballers or actors so that they can make out they're regular customers.

'Why did they come here?' I looked around with disdain.

'They were all friends of Mario.'

'Who?'

'Mario. The owner. Mario Di Angelo.' He said it impatiently like I was slow. The name rang a bell.

'Who's that?'

'The senator. He owns TV Sogni.'

'And he owns this place?'

'Sure. Has done ever since I came to work here thirty years ago. Whenever he wanted to throw a party, he would do it here. Used to bring all his showbiz friends along, all their girls.'

'That so?'

'He knew the meaning of the word largesse. He used to pay for everything. He's the most generous man, always giving presents to people, always offering to do something for you. He looks after everyone. Makes sure everyone's having a good time.'

'That why he went into politics?'

He heard the sarcasm and his face dropped once more. He looked older and more tired suddenly.

'Give me that fifty and I can go back to bed.'

'Why did the parties stop?'

He looked pensive for once. He was staring at the floor and brought his shoulders up to his ears. 'They didn't stop,' he said slowly, 'they just moved elsewhere. A man like Mario isn't one to slow down, believe me.' He smiled, still staring at the floor. Then he snapped out of the reminiscence and put his hand out for his money. I handed over fifty.

'Call me if you see Mori or the girl again and I'll make it two hundred.' I wrote down my number and gave it to him. He grunted and shuffled towards the door to let me out. As I went out into the cold air I heard him twisting the key in the lock.

I walked to the other side of the street and looked back at the hotel. From the outside it looked a little less unattractive. There were plants cascading from one or two balconies. The awning over the entrance was lined by thin fairy lights. I couldn't imagine the place full of A-listers and flowers, but it wasn't as bad outside as it was in.

The night was just beginning to give way to the day. The black was going grey, and there was a faint light in the sky back towards Rome. I could hear birds beginning to chirp and I felt suddenly very tired. Dawn usually has that effect on me. Makes me realise that I haven't been to bed.

I drove the short distance towards the sea with the windows down. The rich smell of salt and seaweed led me towards a wild sandy beach. Strong grasses were growing in the dunes and I parked up on a gravel clearing by a single lifebelt hanging from a wooden post. I reclined the seat and closed my eyes. The sound of the waves breaking on the sand was blissful. Even the squawk of the gulls was somehow soothing, a reminder of raw nature after a night in the city of ancient stones and asphalt. I fell asleep almost immediately. A deep, dreamless sleep.

By the time I woke up it was already hot. It was only eight, but the heat was close. I was sweating. There was a dog barking somewhere on the beach, repeatedly yapping as if it had found something interesting and wanted to let the world know about it. I put my hand to the side of the seat and pulled up the lever, bringing the seat back up to vertical. I looked out at the sea, at the gentle waves as they caressed the sand. There were birds skipping along the shore trying to find food, others gliding on the morning breeze above them. I got out of the car and walked towards the sea, watching my long shadow as it bounced over the dunes and towards the birds. I could see the dog now, digging furiously at something in the sand. The air was reminiscent of those long summers I used to have with my grandparents years ago on the Adriatic: seaweed and salt and damp sand. I stood there for five minutes, thinking about everything and nothing.

Then I turned round, got back in the car and headed towards Viterbo.

It was a slow drive. The Rome rush hour was just starting and I sat in loud, slow traffic as I tried to head north. I put on the radio and listened to some station that was taking calls about a controversial derby match between Lazio and Roma. I couldn't remember a derby that didn't have controversy. Callers were offering each other colourful, raucous insults as they defended their partisan interpretations of last night's game.

Once I was off the ring-road I sped towards Viterbo. If Mori was there, I didn't want to miss him. On the outskirts of town, I stopped at a bar and sank a coffee.

'Via della Salute?' The barman stared at the ceiling, shaking his head. He took out a local directory and found it in the index. 'Ecco,' he said, finding the right page and passing it over the counter.

I got back in the car and found the place easily enough. It was a sad sort of street, lined on both sides by tall blocks from the 1960s. I couldn't see any vegetation other than the weeds growing up through the cracked pavements. The odd balcony had plants and flowers, but there was mostly concrete as far as the eye could see. On all the rooftops there were aerials like bleak silhouetted saplings in winter. Some of the aerials had fallen over and become entangled in the rest of the forest while others looked like old scars, with short lines perpendicular to the main central vane.

Number 34 was towards the far end. There was a rectangle with fifty or sixty surnames. I found Mori's name and held his buzzer. I looked at my watch. It was just after nine.

'Who is it?' a voice said over the intercom.

'My name's Castagnetti. I'm looking for Massimo Mori.'

'That's me. What do you want?'

It felt all too easy. 'I'm looking for a young girl. Simona Biondi. You were staying in a hotel on the outskirts of Rome with her last night.'

'You must have the wrong person.'

'May I come in?'

'You've got the wrong person,' he repeated.

I thought there was a hint of doubt in his voice. 'Can we talk face to face?' I asked.

He hesitated and then buzzed the gate open. 'Ninth floor,' he said.

I walked through the concrete courtyard and into the main foyer. I waited for the lift with a young woman carrying a baby.

'Do you know Massimo Mori?' I asked her. 'He lives on the ninth floor.'

She shrugged and shook her head. 'Don't know any of the neighbours,' she said.

We got in the lift together and the narrow box creaked up to the ninth floor. When the lift doors opened I saw a short man standing in a doorway. He looked the same as the man from the passport: he was the wrong side of middle age with short silver hair, a face lined by the sun and, judging by the smell, cigarettes. His chin had given up the fight against gravity and was covering the top of his jumper. I knew instinctively that he wasn't the man I was looking for. He was in slippers and had something about him that suggested he didn't often get out of them.

'I'm Mori,' he said, holding out a hand.

'Castagnetti.'

'Prego,' he said politely, holding open his door and inviting me inside. 'What's this about?'

We stood facing each other in the corridor. A woman came and stood beside him: she had the same sort of figure and looked, as much as I could tell, like a kindly grandmother: her grey hair was in a bun and she had heirloom glasses balancing on her thin nose.

I pulled the copy of his passport from my pocket and passed it over to him. 'You checked out of the Hotel del Fiume yesterday.'

His glasses were hanging on a chain around his neck and he put them on, looking down his nose at the sheet of paper. He shook his head. 'I've been here all week. Haven't been to Rome at all.'

'May I see your passport?'

He frowned, pulling off his glasses. He raised his white eyebrows as if he suddenly understood what was happening. He was still looking at me when he shut his eyes and shook his head, smiling wryly.

'Where's your passport?'

'I lent it to my brother,' he said. 'Our mother died recently. Well, quite a few months ago now. We've spent a very long time trying to do probate, trying to organise everything. You know what it's like.'

I did, sort of. My parents had checked out when I was still

a kid. I hadn't had to deal with the paperwork, but I had dealt with all the rest.

'Endless forms,' he shook his head, 'and documents. Dealing with lawyers and banks and notaries. It's taken a long time.' He looked at me with a sad, mournful face. 'My brother and I have been slowly going through it all and quite often we've needed ID for this or that. I lent him my passport a month or so ago. I didn't need it after all. The furthest we go nowadays is to the supermarket.'

'What's your brother called?'

'Fabrizio. Fabrizio Mori.'

'And where does he live?'

'South of Rome.'

The three of us stared at each other.

'Can I offer you a coffee?' the old woman asked.

I said I would be grateful and she shuffled off down the corridor.

'Prego, prego,' the man said, leading me into a sitting room. 'Prego,' he said again, motioning towards a low sofa that was upholstered with the thick brown cloth that was fashionable in the 1970s.

'Tell me about your brother,' I said quietly.

He sighed wearily. 'He's always been . . . ' He stopped and stared at the small rectangles of parquet flooring. 'He's always been in trouble. Always.'

'What kind of trouble?'

He shrugged. 'Money trouble. Women trouble. Career trouble. Trouble seems to follow him around as surely as his shadow. Even when we were at school he would get into scrapes. I was nine when he was born so I remember it all. He kept us up all night when he was a baby and he's kept us up ever since.'

I was surprised how respectable the man looked, how formal he seemed. He looked an unlikely sibling of a kidnapper. He looked up at me as if he had read my thoughts and shrugged.

'We may look alike, but we had different fathers. After she was widowed my mother was briefly married to a man. I knew he was a thug. My mother found out pretty fast too, but by then she was pregnant with Fabrizio. The man left before he was even born, which is why he ended up with the same surname as me. Mother tried to wipe the man from her memory, but every time Fabrizio got into trouble she was reminded of her mistake.'

'What kind of scrapes?'

He snorted, a sort of regretful laugh. 'It would have been easier to keep a cat in a pool than keep Fabrizio in a classroom. Every day the school would phone up to say he was absent. "But I took him into the classroom myself," my mother would say. But he had gone to the loo and not come back. Or had gone to a bar and not returned. In the end the school forgot about him and the authorities started taking an interest. He was shoplifting, drinking. You know, the normal alternatives to education.'

The wife came in, bring a tray of small cups and a plate of thin biscuits.

'What's his line of work?' I asked as I spooned sugar into the coffee.

The woman rocked her head to one side, as if to suggest it was an optimistic question.

'He calls himself a photographer.' The man did a slow-motion blink as though he didn't believe it.

'Where?'

'He's self-employed. More self than employed.'

'So how does he earn money?'

The wife was being quiet, clearly not wanting to insult her brother's family, but her disdainful expression was eloquent enough.

'He doesn't,' the older brother said. 'He gets by doing wedding snaps, doing portraits of kids, that sort of stuff. But hardly anything. I would say he gets a commission once a month, if that. And his reputation unfortunately goes before him: that he takes the money and runs. Or that he will only get round to producing the photos when the happy couple already have three children.'

'You said he sometimes does kids' portraits. Has he ever been in trouble with children?'

'How do you mean?' The man's honest eyes looked beady.

'The girl who has gone missing is a very young woman. I don't understand the motive for her abduction as yet, but I'm looking at all the options.'

The man was still staring at me. I could see his wife out of the corner of my eye shaking her head.

'Fabrizio,' he said wearily, 'is lazy, naïve, greedy, even dishonest. That's all true.' The brother was holding his coffee cup at an angle to peer at the remains. 'But he's not that sort. He's never been in trouble with children.'

I nodded, letting him know I trusted his word. 'So what kind of trouble has he been in? And I'm not talking truancy.'

'It would be quicker to say what trouble hasn't he been in.' He gave me a long list of petty offences. It all made Fabrizio Mori sound small fry, the sort of person who didn't have the

43

will or the head to go straight, but didn't have the guile or skill to avoid arrest. He was, like most I had met, in that large middle ground occupied by incompetent crooks.

As Massimo, the older brother, was talking I slowly realised how Fabrizio's troubles had hurt him. Not just the money borrowed and never returned, or the trust betrayed, or the night-time phone calls from various tight spots or holding cells. It was as if having Fabrizio as his younger brother had prevented Massimo from ever entirely being the respectable citizen he craved to be. He was forever associated with his hapless, dishonest half-brother. And because he was only a half-brother, he constantly reminded Massimo of his own father's absence. And now, worst of all, his mourning for his mother was interrupted by the revelation that Fabrizio, rather than sorting out her estate, was involved in the abduction of a young girl.

'So I suppose his name's been in the papers?' I asked.

'Not really. His name only got in the papers when he tried to put other people's in there.'

'What do you mean?'

He rolled his eyes. 'Fabrizio went through a phase when he thought he was a paparazzo. You know, a showbiz snapper, a telephoto snooper. It kind of brought his talents, such as they were, together. He would hang out in fashionable clubs and bars in Rome, stay up all night for one shot of a politician's girl-friend, that sort of nonsense. But he stuck at it. He was good at it. It was the one phase of his life he seemed proud of what he was doing.'

'He used to come round here,' the wife said brightly, relieved to have the chance to speak well of her brother-in-law, 'and show us his photographs. The published versions, I mean. He would bring round a copy of this or that magazine for us. You know, the kind you find at the hairdresser's. And there, in a corner of the page, would be his credit, his name. I'll never forget the first time he showed me one. His name was written so small I could barely see it. It wasn't much, but he was proud of his little achievements and he was desperate for us to share his pride. And we did. It wasn't exactly heroic work, but it was honest and that, by then, was a relief.'

She paused, looking wistfully at the tray of empty coffee cups.

They both seemed reluctant to go on.

'So?'

The husband closed his eyes and shook his head. 'Fabrizio realised he could make more money from people who didn't want to appear in gossip magazines than from those who did.'

'How do you mean?'

'Say what you like about Fabrizio, he always saw an opening. After a few months of snapping these semi-celebrities, he realised he was boosting their careers more than his. The magazine he worked for only bought the flattering shots, the ones where their make-up was perfect, where they were smiling and cheerful.'

The man was hedging around what had happened, not wanting to recall or share his brother's scam.

'So Fabrizio started a collection of more compromising shots. Not just ones where these people looked less glamorous, but photographs in which they were . . .' He paused, lost for words, 'indulging their vices.'

'Meaning?'

He looked at the ceiling briefly, like something up there

could give him strength. 'It was private stuff. Private moments that these people didn't want made public. Fabrizio maybe saw a celebrity out on the town with a lover and would snap all evening. Maybe see a sportsman taking drugs and...' He lowered his index finger like someone snapping away and pulled a disdainful grimace. 'He would find the daughter of a famous industrialist getting passionate in a car and get his shots. I don't know how he even knew where to look. Fabrizio was effectively blackmailing them. I don't think he ever realised that's what he was doing. He said he was just offering his photographs to the highest bidder. Only, of course, the highest bidder was always the compromised person. He started making a lot of money. Significant amounts of money. He stopped coming round here to show us his tiny credits in cheap magazines. In fact, the magazines weren't even publishing his photos any more. He had found a better way to make money.'

The wife sighed and stood up, taking the tray of empty coffee cups back into the kitchen. Mori looked at me and rocked his head slowly, looking at me to make sure it had all sunk in.

'How did he get found out?'

'One of his victims denounced him. Fabrizio was put on trial, convicted of extortion.'

'How long ago was this?'

'Twenty years ago maybe. I can't remember. He spent a few months in prison and then sort of spiralled downhill from there. He had made a lot of money from his little racket but that all disappeared quickly enough. With his reputation, he couldn't get a proper job and, even if he had, he wouldn't have been able to hold it down. At least before he had some energy and charisma, such as it was. For the last few years he's . . .' Mori shrugged as he left the sentence unfinished.

'Where does he live?'

'Campeggio del Sole. It's one of those campsites to the south of the capital. He lives in a static caravan out there. Lot 37 South.'

'You got a phone number?'

I dialled as he said the numbers. There was no reply. I let it ring on as I turned back towards Massimo Mori.

'A young girl is missing and it seems certain she's with your brother. I need to understand what sort of threat he poses. Is he likely to harm her?'

Mori closed his eyes and shook his head. 'No.'

'Presumably you didn't think he would steal or extort either?'

He stared at me. 'You're wrong. I'm afraid I wasn't even surprised when he was arrested for this or that. Not surprised. But he wouldn't, wouldn't ever . . .' He trailed off again, staring at the wall behind me as he shook his head.

'Does the name Simona Biondi mean anything to you?'

He shook his head again. 'Who's that?'

'The girl. Fabrizio's never been connected with anyone called Biondi?'

'Not that I know.'

'Have you got a photograph of him?'

'Of Fabrizio?'

I nodded and he stood up, groaning slightly with the effort as he pushed himself up by leaning on the arm of his chair. He came back a minute later, holding a framed photograph. He passed it over and I looked at the two brothers, arms around each other's shoulders. Fabrizio's face looked longer than his older brother's. He was staring at the camera as if it had insulted him and he looked surly, his eyelids low over his dark, shrewd eyes.

'Nothing more recent?' I asked. The photo I was looking at must have been from twenty years ago.

He shook his head. 'We haven't exactly met up much recently. And even when we do, we don't take snaps for the family album.'

'Mind if I take this?' I asked.

He shrugged as if it were all the same to him. I opened up the back of the frame and slipped out the photo. I tried to imagine him with grey hair in a ponytail.

I gave the man a card and told him to call me if he heard from his brother. He looked at it wearily, like he had been told something similar many times before. He walked me to the door and shook my hand. He looked sheepish, as if he were to blame for his brother's conduct.

'When you find him, tell him to give me my passport back.'

I nodded, thanked him for the coffee, and headed down the nine flights of stairs.

By now the sun was high and hot. The car felt like a sauna as I got in, a gust of dense air hitting me as I bent into the scalding seat. I wound down the windows and drove as fast as I could to get some cool air coming in.

The road to Rome was snarled up as usual. One lane was closed, so cars were aggressively cutting into the remaining one at the last minute to get ahead. I flicked on the radio and heard the same discussion about football that I had heard earlier. I searched for another station and found some Roman reggae. It suited the sunshine and I put my elbow out of the window.

The countryside south of the city was beautiful. I drove past vineyards, large lakes and distant hill towns. And, in between, the scars of industrialisation: old quarries and oil depots and forgotten railways. Rubbish had been dumped randomly and plastic bags hung in the trees, shredding in the wind and turning grey. Eventually the road ran alongside a dense dark pine grove and I saw a sign to the campsite.

It was more like a poor man's suburb than a campsite. Caravans had been parked there for so long that most of the wheels had been replaced by bricks, and permanent patios and hedges had grown up around them. Awnings and tarpaulins were pulled tight over scaffolding poles with elastic bungees. There were neat sets of plastic chairs under each awning and football flags flying from spare poles. As I walked along the gravel path between the caravans I could see that some people had put plastic roses in their hedges. There were people walking around in towelling dressing gowns, ambling back from the communal showers. There were pollarded poplars shading the various lots and, as I looked for Lot 37 South, I could see a concrete ping-pong table, its bumpy surface painted green and white, with Sellotape pulled between two pencils for a net. It was all a strange combination of permanence and improvisation.

I found Fabrizio Mori's place easily enough. It seemed the same as all the others: a shaded shack that looked like it had been parked there twenty years ago and hadn't moved since. There was a padlocked wooden building in the corner of the tiny plot. I peered in through a window and saw a few old tools – some shears and secateurs – and a dozen brown-glass bottles. I turned back towards the caravan and knocked hard on the door. The whole vehicle seemed to wobble as I knocked again. Nothing.

To the side there was only half a metre between the end of the caravan and a green lattice fence. I turned sideways, shuffled down the narrow space and immediately saw a broken window. There were shards of glass on the pillow of the bed in-side.

'Mori,' I called. 'Simona.' No reply. I called again to make sure. Still no reply.

There was an old newspaper caught against the deflated tyre of a bicycle. I used it to knock over the vertical triangles of broken glass still in the window frame and then placed it over the shattered stumps and pulled myself inside.

As soon as I landed the other side I saw something rushing

towards me from the left. A heavy object slammed into the back of my head and knocked me to the side of the bed. The same object hit me again and I fell off the mattress. As I lay on all fours I got kicked in my midriff and collapsed on my side. The kicks kept coming hard. I put my arms over my stomach to protect myself, and I watched the black boots pounding into my forearms.

Eventually the panting animal stepped back. The back of my head was throbbing badly from where I had taken the blow, but I tried to lift it up to see the assailant.

'Who are you?' he grunted. There was a lean authority in his voice.

I pushed myself backwards so I was leaning against the wall. I could feel a patch of warm sticky blood behind my ear. 'Father Christmas,' I said. 'I couldn't find the chimney.'

We stared at each other as he lit a cigarette. He was short and fat. He had a puffy face, like he had eaten too many pastries washed down with sweet wine. His head was bald but for over-length, slightly curly hanks of grey at the sides and there were beads of sweat across his scalp. His shirt, with its improbable floral pattern, was unbuttoned to half-way down his protruding stomach. In his left hand he was holding a long wooden club. His trousers were cream linen, making him look as though he had just stepped off a yacht in the harbour. He smelt of sweat and perfume, like a zoo animal that had just been shampooed. Only his footwear, leather boots with toecaps so circular they must have been steel, gave the impression that he really meant business.

'What are you doing here?' he asked after a couple of deep drags.

'Dropping off presents.'

'Don't play the wise guy,' he whispered. He took a step towards me and put his shoe on the knuckles of my right hand. He bent down and held the orange tip of the cigarette an inch from my eye. 'What are you doing here?'

'I'm trying to find a girl.'

'Who?' He straightened up, still staring at me with his mouth twisted in disdain.

'Simona Biondi.' I tried to push myself up. 'That name mean anything to you?'

'Why come here?'

'She's been abducted by Fabrizio Mori.'

'That so?' he asked disinterestedly. 'And who are you?'

I pushed myself to my feet. My head was still throbbing and I rolled it round my shoulders, keeping my eyes on the thug. 'Castagnetti. I'm a private detective.'

'Who hired you?'

'The parents of the missing girl.'

He looked at me through narrowed eyes. He took one last drag on his cigarette and then flicked it out of the broken window. 'You won't find anything here.'

'I found you.'

He snorted in derision as if he were small fry. It looked like a sign of weakness and I tried to exploit it.

'What are you doing here?' I asked.

'Same as you. Been hired by someone to find Mori.'

'Why?'

He shook his head. 'Just got to find him. That's all I know.'

'Who hired you?'

He clicked his tongue, tutting away the question. The moment of weakness was gone.

'Mind if I look around?'

'There's nothing here.'

He was blocking my way, standing between the end of the bed and the wall. I shook some glass off the pillow and sat down on it. I put my head between my knees and looked underneath the bed. There were a lot of boxes down there, a grey T-shirt, a cobwebbed sock. I pulled one of the boxes out and rifled through it briefly: it was mostly copies of old gossip magazines. I lifted them above the bed and dropped them onto the thin mattress. Dust billowed in all directions. Magazines fanned out across the faded floral sheets. I pushed them apart and looked at one or two covers: the smiles of the eager girls on the covers looked strange behind the dust, like they were dated and their moment had passed. Their glamour looked long gone.

On the white plastic bedside table I saw the issue of *Moda* in which Simona's photograph had appeared. I flicked through until I found her and passed it over to the man.

'There,' I said to the thug, 'that's the girl I'm looking for.'

He took the magazine and leered at her. 'Nice piece.'

The other boxes were the same: more gossip magazines, older this time. The stars were different but the poses and the pouts were the same. I leafed through them quickly, trying to find anything or anyone that might help.

Next to me the man picked up a copy at random and leafed through it. 'That man was a cretin,' he said, looking at a snap of a man in a black shirt and black suit. He threw the magazine down and picked up another. 'Sweet little piece she was. She was always going to rise to the top.'

'You know these people?'

'Sure. Most of them.'

I looked at him again. His bare chest was smooth and sun-tanned. He looked like a bull who hung out with the peacocks.

'How come?'

'I work in the industry.'

'Which industry?'

He threw his chin at the pile of magazines fanned across the mattress. 'That one,' he said disparagingly. 'The gossip industry. Showbiz.' He grinned for the first time and I saw that one of his front teeth was gold-plated. 'I work for one of the big TV stations.'

'Which one?'

He looked at me with his head on one side, weighing up whether to spill or not. Pride got the better of him. 'TV Sogni.'

'Quite a comedown to breaking into caravans and beating up members of the public.'

He looked at me and bounced his head to one side. 'All part of my job.'

'And what's that exactly?'

He just tutted again, refusing to answer. I looked at him again and smiled derisively. In the world of showbiz he might have passed for a hard man, but I had seen much harder. His only advantages were surprise and a wooden club, and the first was gone.

I barged past him and went to the other end of the caravan. It wasn't far. There was a tiny kitchen with two hot-rings and a rickety oven. I opened the cupboards and saw only a few sticky plates and plastic cups. Behind me was a narrow bath-room. I went through it but found nothing. Beyond that was a sitting area. Rigid rectangular cushions were placed at right angles to make an uncomfortable sofa. I lifted them and looked through the chests underneath. In one there were old clothes and photographic magazines and the usual debris of life: a snorkel, a few paperbacks, old cassettes, a biscuit tin containing spare washers and nuts.

I dropped the lid and went over to the other chest, taking off the cushion and looking underneath. There was more of the same: a rucksack, old bills from Telecom Italia, a rusty pair of scissors. But at the bottom was a metal box. It was dented and dark brown. A padlock knocked against the metal as I lifted it out.

The thug was standing behind me now, watching. I told him to find the key.

He grunted and started going through drawers again. I heard cutlery and coat hangers rattling. He came back a minute later, shrugging and shaking his head.

We both stared at the box feeling impotent. The thug took the padlock in his hands as if weighing it.

I watched him climb back out of the broken bedroom win-dow. He came back two minutes later with some heavy-duty bolt cutters. The handles were almost a metre long. He placed the teeth over the thin metal of the padlock and it gave a dull snap as it broke. He threw the lock on the floor and pulled out thick piles of photographs in each hand. He passed me a hand-ful as the snaps slipped apart. Even from the corners I could see naked limbs.

'Shit,' he said under his breath. 'This guy has the dirt on everybody.'

I went through my pile and each one was a variation on a theme: couples embracing, kissing, dancing, snorting, screwing. Some of the snaps were out of focus or blurred, others were clearly taken from a long distance away and were at odd angles.

The man next to me was muttering appreciation for the passion on display. 'Little whore,' he said. 'I always knew she was filthy.'

'Who are these people?' I asked.

'Same people you saw in those magazines in there,' he thumbed over his shoulder at the pile of magazines on the bed. 'Same people, different poses.'

These were the compromising photos that Mori had used to blackmail various celebrities, just as his brother had said. This sort of archive must have been worth a few million lire back in the day.

'Was he blackmailing all of these people?' I asked.

The man was still looking at the photographs. He didn't reply.

'How did he get caught? I hear he did time for extortion.'

He looked at me now, throwing the snaps down onto the narrow table between the two sofas. These sordid photos seemed to have made us into allies somehow, like we were both voyeurs who were unexpectedly on the same side. We were both looking at the same thing in the same way.

'You remember Filippo Marinelli, the footballer?'

I shook my head.

'He used to play for Perugia and then Roma. The poor guy was married, but Mori had photographs of him with another woman. There were apparently drugs involved too, so Mori thought he was onto a nice little earner. He thought he would fleece the rich footballer, who otherwise risked losing his career as well as his wife. But Marinelli had given up on his marriage and was at the end of his career. So he denounced the extortion.'

'And?'

'You know, the usual bull. Mori was arrested, released, re-arrested, tried, imprisoned, acquitted on appeal, released again. The story rumbled on for years. Mori was a piece of shit, but he was smart. He said he was simply selling photographs to the highest bidder, which he was in a way.'

'How do you mean?'

The man looked at me like he was angry at being pumped for information. But he shrugged and looked away, as if everyone knew the story anyway. 'Mori was working with a magazine sub editor. The sub used to call up the victim and say, all cosy and friendly, "Look, I don't want you to get into trouble, so I thought you should know we've got hold of this picture and we're going to run it . . ." And the sub would let slip how much his magazine was going to pay for the snapshot and who was selling. So the victim, of course, got hold of Mori and offered more. And Mori would then split the sum with the sub. It was a decent scam. And even when he got rumbled he had enough dirt on enough people to persuade everyone to go easy on him. Look.' He picked up a few photos at random. 'He had the dirt on politicians, businessmen, magistrates, everyone. He was attracted to the dirt like a fly to the shit. It's hardly surprising they all went easy on him when it came to court.'

'When did all this happen?'

'Huh,' he threw his head back. 'Long, long time ago.'

'And then?'

'I never heard of him again until this morning. All I know is I was told to come here and bring him in.'

'By who?'

He stared at me. 'You ask too many questions.'

I had a lot more I hadn't asked him. Like whether there was a connection between him looking for Mori and me looking for Simona Biondi. It was the sort of coincidence that set me thinking. And if there was a connection, I needed to know what it was. My guess was that this thug was working for someone who was being blackmailed by Mori, and the Biondi girl was somehow involved. Maybe she had the dirt on someone too. Maybe she was the dirt.

'Where do you reckon he's heading?' the man asked me. He looked lost, like the kind of man who wasn't used to asking advice and felt a fool for doing so.

'I expect he's heading straight for the person who hired you.'

He nodded to say that he understood.

'You want to tell me who that is?'

'He's a very private man.'

'You mean he's got a hyperactive private life.'

He smiled slightly, a leery kind of smile. 'Yeah, he likes his private life.'

'And what were you supposed to do when you found Mori?'

'Bring him in.'

It was the kind of phrase that could cover a range of solutions.

I went over to the kitchen corner and found a large pan. I threw some of the rags from the chest in it.

'Give me your lighter,' I said.

'What are you doing?'

'Give.'

He passed over a heavy silver lighter. The flame was high and the rags took quickly. I began feeding in the photos, one after the other. Images of bare flesh wrinkled and turned black. Moments of passion turned into ashes. It stank bad, but it felt good.

'What are you doing?' he said again. 'That stuff is worth a fortune.'

'You want to go into the same game as Mori?'

'I'd play it better.' He picked up one of the snaps and turned it sideways. 'Look, that guy's in parliament. Think what he would pay you to do what you're doing now.'

'I like doing it for free.'

He threw it in the pan with the others. 'Just seems like a waste, that's all. There are more secrets here than in the Vatican.'

I looked at each snap as I threw it into the fire. The photos kept curling black as they burnt to nothing.

'It's been a pleasure,' I said to the man. 'See you around.'

'Where you going? Where's Mori?'

'I've no idea. I'm not looking for him. I'm after Simona Biondi.' I walked off and squeezed back out of the broken window. The campsite was the same as before, only busier. I could see people in flip-flops heading off to the beach. The sun was up high and there were tiny lizards darting between the stones. I could smell a rich sauce that someone was already simmering for lunch. I realised I hadn't eaten for a long time and could feel my stomach tightening around nothing. I got in the car and went to look for some food.

I made a few phone calls as I sat in the restaurant waiting for the bill. It was one of those places that looked down at heel, but only because it hadn't been done up for a few decades. The food was perfect and the place was full of customers noisily talking to old friends across the tables. I needed to find out where Filippo Marinelli was living. I called in a favour from a low-ranking carabiniere who put me in touch with someone else and by the time they had brought the bill – it seemed wrong it was so low – I had an address.

I headed back to Rome. I drove with the window down, feeling the warm air gusting in like a wide-angle hairdryer. The fields round here were dotted with ancient ruins, stones that had stood there for thousands of years. There were sheep huddling in the shade of ancient Roman walls, weeds growing out of long-lost settlements. Rome always felt like this to me: a place where the grandeur of an empire had slipped away centuries ago, but one that still retained hints of that lost magnificence. Even meandering livestock lived in the shadow of that great civilisation and we moderns somehow knew we could never emulate, let alone surpass, it. That was what it was like here: it was a constant reminder of past glories and present inadequacies.

I came to a smart suburb where the shops were shaded by large trees. I could hear the clatter of cutlery as a waiter cleared the outside tables of a restaurant that had bright orange tablecloths. It was clearly an elegant suburb: even the pharmacy, I saw through the window, had long, leather sofas for its waiting customers.

Marinelli's house was just round the corner from the chic shops. The villa looked large and immaculate. There were stone balconies outside every window with ornate, slightly convex iron railings covered with wisteria. There was a convertible BMW in the drive parked between large, stone sculptures of eagles.

I rang the buzzer.

'Who is it?'

'My name's Castagnetti. I'm a private investigator.'

'What do you want?'

'I was hoping to ask you a couple of questions.'

'About what?'

'It's a delicate subject. A girl has gone missing.'

'What's that got to do with me?'

'Can we talk face to face?'

I heard a click and then saw the large gate sliding back. As soon as it did so, two large Alsatians ran towards me, stopping a metre in front of me and lowering their heads to bark madly as they bared their wet, yellow teeth.

A man appeared at the door of the villa fifty metres away and shouted aggressively at the dogs. They ignored him, continuing to snarl at me, until he shouted again and they slowly retreated, occasionally turning round to offer a half-hearted bark to register their protest at my intrusion.

The man was walking towards me now. He looked about fifty and had salt and pepper hair. He looked fit, wearing trainers and shorts and a black Lacoste top. He was tanned and good-looking.

'Sorry about the dogs. They're not very hospitable.' He pointed towards me. 'They didn't do that, did they?'

'What?'

'You're limping.'

'No, that's an old injury.' We shook hands. 'I'm Castagnetti.'

'Marinelli. Come in.'

The place was immaculate but sterile. It felt like it wasn't lived in, as if there were more money than warmth here. It reminded me of the Biondi pad. Every surface was shiny: the hall floor was a dark, polished wood, the walls had large mirrors, the hall table was a long slab of granite.

'Coffee?' he asked.

We walked into the kitchen and he put the two halves of the hour-glass of metal together.

'You want to tell me what this is all about?' He stared at me. There was something about his manner that was direct and honest, like he wanted everything out in the open. I don't know why but I liked him.

'Like I said, I'm an investigator. I've been hired by two distraught parents to look for their young daughter.'

He nodded as he took a cloth and wiped up a few fallen coffee grounds. 'What's that got to do with me?'

'The man who abducted her is someone you've . . .' I paused, trying to think of the tactful way to say it, 'had trouble with in the past.'

He looked at me and raised his eyebrows. 'Who?'

'Fabrizio Mori.'

His eyes narrowed and he nodded slowly. 'Mori, eh?' He lit

the gas under the coffee maker and opened a cupboard door to pull out two little white cups. 'I don't really see how I can help you. That was a long time ago.'

'I haven't got much else to go on.' I held his stare. 'I'm contacting anyone who might be able to help me find that girl.'

He nodded. 'How old is she?'

'Only eighteen.'

'And she's definitely with Mori?'

'Seems that way.'

He smiled as if he were in pain. 'He always was a piece of shit. If I hadn't taken him on he would still be snapping away, blackmailing anyone with a secret this side of Istanbul. He was the worst sort of hustler.'

'I heard you were one of his victims.'

He nodded. 'I was playing for Roma at the time.' He glazed over, as if he were either bored or nostalgic. 'I had just broken into the first team and had scored a couple of goals. When that happens, you find that every time you go out there's a queue of women wanting to throw themselves at you.' He smiled ruefully. 'My marriage was over by then anyway. My wife had had a fling with one of my team-mates, a guy from the same part of France as her. Everyone knew about it. So one night I went out and met a girl. She was uninhibited, but like I said, when you're a footballer, you don't meet girls who aren't. She was forward, and we ended up, you know . . .'

Behind him I could see a huge plasma screen on the wall. He looked like the kind of bachelor who had remote controls for company. The coffee roared its arrival and he poured it out. He took the cups on their little saucers over to a kitchen island and motioned me to sit down on one of the designer stools. It had a small black leather seat and a tiny leather backrest. There was a circle of metal towards the bottom to rest your feet on. It felt like balancing on a toothpick.

'Then what happened?'

'A few weeks later I got a call from a friend of mine. I thought he was a friend. A guy who used to work on one of those glossy mags about the rich and famous. He'd run a couple of decent stories about me in the past, you know, photo shoots of me at home playing the happy family man, touting me as a future captain of his country. You know, really puffing me up. He and I had had a couple of drinks now and then.' He spooned some sugar into his cup and stirred it slowly, looking at the brown liquid before knocking it back. 'So he phoned me up and said he wanted to warn me of something they had got hold of. Some photographer was touting around photos of me doing lines of coke with a topless girl. He said he thought I should know and did I want him to put me in touch with the photographer. He suggested I could make a higher bid for the snaps to keep them out of the public domain.'

'And?'

'I got the photographer's name and took it to the police.'

'That was brave.'

'My marriage was over anyway, and everyone else I knew was doing similar things. I underestimated the hypocrisy. I was sacked and dropped down the leagues.'

'And Mori did time?'

'A bit. He had made enough money to make it worthwhile, from what I heard.'

'Not from what I've seen.'

He looked up at me. 'What do you mean?'

'He's living in a caravan site a two-hour bus ride out of town.'

'Like I said, this was twenty years ago. I'm sure he's spent it since then.'

A young woman came into the kitchen looking like she had just got out of bed. She was wearing a thin cotton nightgown so you could see the silhouette of her perfect figure against the light.

'My daughter,' Marinelli said under his breath.

She ignored us, but must have been aware of our presence since she put a hand self-consciously into her slept-on hair. She made some toast and opened the fridge to get some butter. She took out the milk and poured herself a large glass, and then put the lot on a tray and left.

'I barely saw her as a child,' Marinelli said wistfully. 'It's like we're living in this house as strangers, not sure how to treat each other. I think she sees me as a cheap hotel.'

'All children do.'

'Yeah.' He smiled. 'It's just I'm not used to it. Her mother left soon after the scandal, they went home. I took a job out there coaching when I retired, you know, to be close to her, but she doesn't even remember it.' He stared at the wall. 'You can hardly blame her. I came back here after a year as my mother was dying. In the space of a few years I lost everything.' He stared at me with a grim, embittered expression. 'Career, wife, daughter, mother.'

'And it was Mori that took it from you.'

He looked upwards and sighed. 'I took it from myself. I threw it away.' He was shaking his head. 'That's what everyone does in their twenties – with money, with love, with whatever. Only most people that age don't have everything: the children possibly, but not the beautiful wife and certainly not the money. A footballer does, he has it all in his teens if he's lucky, and it's all over so soon. I just didn't know what I had. I threw it away.'

'Mori played his part.'

Marinelli stared at me and realised I was trying to provoke him. He nodded slowly. 'Yeah, he was a cunning bastard too. The girl I was with that night, well . . .' He was looking at the floor, frowning slightly. 'She went missing soon afterwards.'

'How do you mean?'

'She went missing,' he said it louder, like I was stupid. 'Anna Sartori was her name. It was all over the papers back in the early nineties. It became quite a story for a while. You know, "nubile escort goes missing". It kind of spooks me now, to think about it.'

'And? What happened?'

'That was it. She was never found.'

We sat there in silence for a while. He was staring at the floor, nodding slowly as if he were rerunning his past in his head.

'And you think Mori was responsible?'

He shrugged without moving his gaze from the matt beige tiles. 'As far as I was concerned, he was capable of anything.'

'But if he was making money from honey traps, why dispose of the honey?'

Marinelli shrugged again. 'They probably fell out. She might have wanted to testify against him. Maybe she knew too many secrets.'

'What was she like, this Anna Sartori?'

'I liked her. She was beautiful, cute. I had no idea she was part of a blackmail scam. And, in a strange way, I don't think she really knew what was going on. When he started asking me for money, I assumed she had been in on the racket with him. And when I ran into her in a club a few months later, I confronted her and told her what I thought of her. I insulted her pretty colourfully and she didn't get it. She looked all confused. It turns out she didn't really understand what was going on herself.'

I frowned. It seemed improbable. He saw my doubt and explained, closing his eyes as he did so.

'Those kind of parties didn't have many rules. There could be a couple making out on the sofa next to you. Someone would pull out a bag of cash or gear. It didn't even seem unusual to me after a while. With all the strobe lights you wouldn't notice someone taking a flash photo. You wouldn't think twice about a topless girl sitting next to you. That's what it was like.'

'So this girl didn't know someone was snapping away?'

He put his chin to one side. 'She knew him, knew that he was taking photos. But she thought it was to promote her, to get her into the papers. That's what all those girls cared about. They would have done anything, anything to get their left ankle in one of those magazines. So she was free and easy, happy to let Mori snap away as she thought that was the way to the big time. She had no idea he was taking photos that people were buying to keep out of magazines. It was the opposite of what she thought was going on. She never thought they were being used for extortion.'

'And you believed her?'

'Yeah, I did. She was furious when she found out. She thought she was putting herself about to get in the papers, to make a name for herself. And actually, she was just there as bait

67

for a shakedown. She was more innocent than that. I know it sounds strange, but she was like a young girl in an adult world. Even the longing to be a showgirl on TV was girlish. She was determined to make it. Determined to be famous, for whatever reason. She would have done anything to fulfil that dream, even all sorts of "adult" things. And she did. Only she didn't know he was snapping it all, making a record of how low she would go and with who. He was using her to make money. Most of those girls demean themselves in the hope of stardom, but don't realise that's all stardom is: it's performing in private. She was never going to make it. He let her think she was getting close, so she would keep on playing his game until, in the end, it was game over.'

'You got a photo of her?'

He laughed bitterly. Given the context it was the wrong thing to ask. 'You could find her face in the papers from around that time.' He shook his head sadly. 'She was beautiful: thick dark hair, dark eyes, dark skin. Everything about her was passionate.'

While he was reminiscing about an old flame that had burnt him, I felt a rising urgency about Simona's well-being. I still had no leads on Mori, but I felt I was getting closer to him, beginning to understand who he was and how he worked. He used murky photographs like chips in a casino, chucking them around until the gamble paid off and someone turned them into a stack of cash. It was a dirty business, the kind of work that would make him a lot of money and even more enemies. I had assumed until now that Mori was up to his old tricks, making money out of people's weaknesses by using beautiful women as bait. I couldn't work out what he wanted with young Simona, but I guessed, unlikely as it seemed, that she was the new honey in the trap. She was the lure. Her parents and sister thought that she wasn't that sort, but parents always think that of their children. If she was desperate to become a starlet, like Anna Sartori, she might have been prepared to play the part Mori wanted. And the fact that the thug in his caravan was after Mori too made me think that he was trying to squeeze cash from someone who had a secret to hide. Someone who had, presumably, hired the thug. It had appeared sordid, but not particularly dangerous. But if one of Mori's girls had gone missing in the past, the stakes were suddenly higher.

'Who was the go-between who brokered the deal?' I asked Marinelli, waking him up from his reverie.

He smiled ruefully again. 'A guy called Gianni Esposito.'

'On what magazine?'

He let out a dismissive sigh. 'I can't remember. No idea. One of the usuals.'

'Ever heard of him since?'

He shook his head. 'He was tried along with Mori. Can't remember what happened to him. Let off I think.'

'Gianni Esposito,' I said quietly. I committed the name to memory, wondering what role, if any, he had in this current case.

We heard the front door open and shut. Marinelli stood up and went to the window. We heard the sound of a moped revving up outside. It grew fainter as he came back to the kitchen table and rolled his eyes.

'Not a word,' he said, shaking his head. 'She won't come back until after midnight and I've no idea where she is, who she's with.'

'Must worry you.'

'Yeah, it does.' It sounded like it made him more angry than worried.

'Simona Biondi,' I said slowly, 'this girl I'm looking for, she hasn't been seen since the day before yesterday. Her parents are very worried. Does that name mean anything to you?'

He suddenly turned to me as if I had woken him up. He shook his head conclusively, quickly. 'Nothing.'

'You've never heard her name before?'

He shook his head again, raising his palms as if to apologise for his ignorance.

I stood up and thanked him for the coffee. He walked me to the door and held it open as the dogs reappeared and snarled. He stared at them angrily, picking up an umbrella from behind the door like it was the only way to let out all his frustration. They yelped pitifully as they retreated. He clicked open the gate for me and I exchanged his cold, perfect house for the hot chaos of the capital.

I walked along the pavement above the Tiber, looking down at the light brown river and the oblique steps descending down to the banks. There were a few boats moored up there, rocking left and right in the breeze. I watched a few squawking gulls as they tried to snatch crumbs from the deck of a pleasure boat. One of the birds got what it wanted and soared up to the rooftops to enjoy its takings. I saw it alight on the top of one of the blocks of flats, disappearing amidst the forest of aerials and satellite dishes.

I stood there, staring at the ugly receivers. Strange that they were the means by which synthetic dreams were captured, that it was those metallic tangles that brought the tinny laughter and forced applause into people's lives. Next to them the white dishes were all facing upwards to the sky as if in admiration of a orbiting god. There was something beseeching about their angle, about that recipient, passive pose, like the viewers themselves, with their gaze cast up to the passing stars.

Back in the city I checked into a hotel near Piazza del Popolo. It was an old-fashioned place, full of dark wood, antiquarian maps and quiet staff. I went up to my room in a slow lift and made some calls. It didn't take long to discover that Gianni Esposito worked on a magazine called *Desire*. I called the publication and they told me that Esposito was in.

I wrote down the address and went round there. It was a short walk outside the centre, where the streets became boulevards and the shops, rather than selling designer outfits, sold discount underwear and cheap suitcases. There were fading posters from some recent political campaign, the politicians' large faces smiling at pedestrians. There were trite slogans written underneath, many of which had been doctored or defaced.

I wondered to myself why I was chasing a story from twenty years ago instead of the current one. I had to follow any leads I found, and if I had none on Simona, then I would chase loose ends from back in the 1990s. I wasn't sure if history was repeating itself, but I knew that as names came up I had to confront them, see what they could tell me about the past and what that might say about the present.

The magazine's offices were in a large block housing various other titles. The ground-floor reception had lime-green sofas

72

and copies of the covers of various magazines from years gone by. There were photographs of couples on snowy mountains, smiling outrageously at something as they stared into the far distance; there were pictures of fashionably dressed children running along the beach holding hands, their feet splashing in the water. I looked for a cover of *Desire* and saw a woman on her hands and knees, showing her cleavage. It was someone I recognised from the TV, but I couldn't place the programme. She looked young and seductive. *The cat with nine lives*, read the headline.

The whole place exuded fantasy. This was what people aspired to: the laughter, the glamour of snowy peaks, feet splashing in a transparent sea, a beautiful wife with perfect teeth and voluptuous curves. On the far wall, in large letters, it said *Sogni Group*.

The woman on the front desk, though, looked like a sourpuss. She was the wrong side of plump, her face was barely symmetrical and her short black hair made her look like the austere adult guardian of these childish fantasies.

'I'm looking for Gianni Esposito,' I said to her.

She raised one eyebrow. 'It's press day today so he'll be very tied up. Have you got an appointment?'

I shook my head.

'Name?'

'Castagnetti. I'm a private investigator.'

She looked at me like she wanted to ask more questions. She picked up the phone instead. 'Someone here to see Gianni,' she barked. 'I know, I know. Shall I send him up anyway?'

I couldn't hear the reply, but when she hung up she nodded towards the lift. 'Eighth floor,' she said.

'All these magazines are part of the Sogni stable, right?'

She nodded.

'Who owns Sogni?'

'Mario Di Angelo. He's got more titles than a medieval monarch.' She didn't smile as she said it, but picked up the phone again, ready to make another call.

I took the lift up to the eighth floor and came out into a reception area with frosted glass doors in all directions. The girl behind the front desk was cute and knew it.

'Can I help you?' she asked.

'I'm here to see Gianni Esposito,' I said.

'He'll be busy all day today. You got an appointment?'

I shook my head. She looked at me like there wasn't a chance, so I showed her a copy of my badge. She looked nonplussed, but stood up and walked through one of the glass doors, moving like she was trying to swat flies with her hips.

I went and sat down, picking up a copy of *Desire*'s latest issue. It only took a couple of minutes to read. It was almost all photos, the usual sort of stuff at this time of year: minor stars sunbathing topless on a distant yacht, some actor who had a new squeeze, a few collages from parties in Sardinia and Forte. I only recognised a couple of the faces or names.

The girl came back and told me that Esposito would see me in a few minutes. She went and sat back at her computer and tapped away. The first time the phone rang she put on a headset so she could answer it without taking her hands off the keyboard. Her voice was from the streets of Rome, a hard, gurgling voice that sounded like it wouldn't take any shit but could certainly dish it out.

It was quarter of an hour before Esposito came in. He had

grey hair cut so short that it was only visible as white specks against his tanned scalp. His face was unnaturally tanned and what looked like a muscular torso was squeezed into a shiny mauve shirt.

'You Castagnetti?'

I stood up and nodded. He held out a hand and he looked at me with curiosity.

'Come on. It's press day. I haven't got much time.'

He walked back the way he had come, expecting me to follow like a faithful dog. He led me into an office with a large plasma screen showing some muted talk show. There were piles of newspapers and invitations and DVDs in all directions. He walked over to a water cooler and filled a small plastic cup. 'What's this about?' He sat behind his desk and motioned with his chin that I should sit on a chair the other side.

'A young girl's gone missing. She's called Simona Biondi. I've been hired to find her.'

He shrugged. 'Who's she?'

'An eighteen-year-old girl.'

He flicked the bottom of a soft packet of cigarettes and put an emerging filter tip in his mouth. 'How can I help?' The cigarette bounced up and down as he spoke.

'She's with a man. Someone you know. Or did. Fabrizio Mori.'

He put his head back, looking at the ceiling. He rolled his jaw left and right so that the thin cigarette moved like the needle of a metronome. He leant forward and flicked open a lighter and brought the flame to the cigarette. 'Mori, eh? Haven't heard of him for twenty years.' He sucked deeply and then turned to the side as he exhaled white smoke. 'You got a photo of this girl?'

I passed over the shot from the magazine.

'Cute. Very cute.' He looked at the paper, turned it over like he recognised the magazine. 'Was she in the business?' He waved a vertical index round the office to imply, I guessed, the world of glamour.

I shook my head. 'Mori saw this snap when it was published and moved in on her. I'm trying to work out why, understand what he saw in her.'

'Probably what most men see in a girl that age.' He said it wistfully, as if he wished men wouldn't waste themselves on young girls.

'Mori was in the blackmailing business. That's how he made his money. Secret snaps of secret vices. I heard you used to help him out.'

Esposito fixed me with a stare and slowly started to smile. 'Is that why you're here? You think I'm something to do with snatching this girl?'

I moved my head left and right. 'No. But I think you were involved in something twenty years ago, and I've got a hunch this case is connected.'

He dragged hard on his cigarette and blew out the smoke like an act of defiance. 'The only mistake I ever made with Mori all those years ago was trying to help out some friends.'

'What does that mean?'

'Listen, sweetie, I get sent snaps all day every day.' He opened a drawer and threw a pile of stills angrily in my direction. I looked through them: naked shots of beautiful women, a man bent over a line of powder, a couple groping in the dark. 'Every day photographers are hustling, trying to get me to buy shots of famous people. Every day I get sent this shit.'

'And?'

'I can make or break someone's career. Put a flattering shot on the cover and they're made. Put one of those somewhere and they're ruined. You follow? I've got enormous power and they know it.'

I raised an eyebrow, waiting for him to finish. He clearly liked his power, the possibilities of playing God with the stars.

'A lot of these people are my friends. These are the people I hang out with.' He ran off a list of names that I sort of recognised. 'We go out together, they invite me to their parties and onto their yachts.'

'So?' I said impatiently.

'When I get sent that sort of shit,' he jutted his chin towards the snaps on my lap, 'I let them know they need to be more discreet. I warn them that someone in their circle is taking the piss.'

'The way I heard it, you were part of a dummy auction for these sort of snaps, upping the price so that Mori made a nice profit and shared it with you.'

His eyelids hung low on his eyes like he was bored with me. He crushed the butt into a large white ashtray and stared at me. 'You heard wrong. I never publish this sort of stuff. Never would. Not unless someone deserves it.'

'What would they have to do to deserve it? Not invite you onto their yacht?'

He threw me an issue of his magazine. 'I made most of these people. Most of them love me for it, but one or two are ungrateful. They forget who made them, who put them up there.'

'And they're the ones you bring low?'

'I'll occasionally publish the truth about them.' He shrugged. 'Mori wanted me to publish compromising shots of some of my close friends. All I did was warn them what he was up to.'

'Filippo Marinelli?'

'Yeah, sure, I called him. Told him some punk was trying to ruin his career. Told him the name of the guy and suggested he keep things a bit more discreet. And for that I was dragged through the courts, subjected to years of judicial bullshit. And I was cleared of all charges. Cleared of all charges,' he said again, more slowly.

The phone rang and he snatched it up. He barked some instructions and slammed the handset down again. He paused, recollected himself and pulled a false smile. 'Are we done?'

'Not quite. Mori was working with a girl called Anna Sartori.'

'Yeah,' he said, his smile turning nasty. 'I remember her.'

'She went missing soon after things blew up.'

'You're not going to blame that on me as well, are you?'

I shrugged. 'You ever meet her?'

He had a look of wry amusement. 'I had seen her in the snaps. Seen quite a lot of her, if you see what I mean. She certainly put herself about, didn't she?'

'You ever meet her?'

He ran a palm across his shaved scalp. 'Sure. Just the once.'

'When was that?'

'Before the so-called scandal broke. She must have known her handler Mori was sending me those snaps and she,' he chuckled quietly to himself, 'wanted to make sure I printed them. You know, most girls wouldn't want those sort of sordid pictures in public, but she was desperate for it, she was sure they were her ticket to the big time. You know, there she was – topless, even naked, cavorting with some politician or footballer. She was shameless. Was desperate for me to run them in the magazine.'

'And you didn't?'

'Of course not. Those people are my friends.' He wagged his index finger as if it were out of the question. 'We deal with glamour here, not pornography.'

'I thought it was all the same.'

His grin was condescending, as though he were surprised he even had to explain to me how things worked. 'Glamour is about dreams, aspirations, lifestyle, fashion . . .'

'Frolics,' I said. 'Fantasies, flesh.'

'No,' he said, shaking his head from one side to the other like he was watching a game of tennis. 'It's about taste. Aesthetics. Those snaps were sordid, the sort of sleaze we're completely opposed to.'

'So she came in here, hoping to persuade you to publish. You gave her your little sermon about glamour – and?'

'She started telling me her life story, how she had come to Rome with Mori and how they had tried to get her into the glamour game. Or that's what she thought he was doing. But she had discovered he was using her, making money by keeping her out of the press rather than getting her into it. She started crying, you know, all the waterworks. I tried to console her.'

'Is that all you did?'

He grinned, showing me his perfect teeth. 'That's not my thing. And that, by the way, is why people trust me. I don't interfere with any of the girls here. I prefer consoling young men, if you follow.'

'So, what happened then?'

'Sartori wanted the same as all of them, wanted to get on TV. I knew the guy who worked as the studio manager over at Di Angelo's station and put them in touch.'

'Who's that?'

'Guy called Tony Vespa.'

'Who's he?'

'He's like the bouncer for the floor shows. He used to be the handler for all those young girls.'

'And he still works for Di Angelo?'

'Sure. Always has, always will. He's been his fixer for decades. His job back then was to find the girls for those crazy shows, to find the dancers and strippers and the like. Normally they would be taken to Di Angelo for vetting, if you know what I mean. He liked to meet them in the flesh. Just the flesh.' He laughed at his little joke.

'So you introduced Anna Sartori to this man Vespa, the fixer at the TV studios?'

'Right. And that was more or less the last I heard of her.'

'Until . . . ?'

'Until I heard she had gone missing.' He stared at his desk as if that was the decent thing to do. 'Anything else?'

'Where will I find Vespa?'

'Vespa?'

'Where does he live?'

Esposito hesitated and then leant forward and slowly rolled a wheel of index cards. I looked at his tanned fingers as he flicked through the cards. He stopped and pulled one out. He held it between his index and middle fingers and offered it over, pulling away when I made a move to take it.

'I'll need something in return.'

'You want to console me too?'

'You're not my type.' He smiled sarcastically. 'I want to know what this is all about, where it goes. You've aroused my curiosity.'

'Or your greed?'

He stared at me, waving the index card in his fingers like he was asking a question.

I shrugged wearily. 'I've told you. A young girl has gone missing. It seems likely she's with Mori. I suspect he's putting the squeeze on someone but I don't know why yet.'

He let me take the index card from his fingers. I looked at the address and passed it back.

'Let me know what you find out, won't you?'

I made a non-committal grunt and let myself out of his office.

'See you around,' I said over my shoulder as I retraced my steps back to the reception and the lift.

The next morning I went round to Tony Vespa's place. It was a small villa that didn't seem finished. It was trying hard to be Beverley Hills, but the result was a suburban building site. The bare bricks were unrendered and what should have been grand columns outside the house were still just steel supports. I rang the doorbell and peered through the window: there was a woman in knickers putting a silk gown on her shoulders.

She opened the door and looked at me. The gown was just hanging loosely on her shoulders so that most of her front was on show. She stood there provocatively, slightly side on so that I could see everything she had.

'What do you want?' she asked, like she was used to trouble. Her accent sounded East European.

'I'm looking for Tony.'

She stepped aside, raising her hand inside the room as if I should come in. The action pulled her robe wide apart so that she might as well have been topless.

I walked past her and smelt the chlorine on her skin. The house looked expensively furnished: long white sofas, a large TV on the wall, a square, glass table with antiques lined up: large pots and dented coins.

'He's by the pool,' the woman said, walking towards me as she belted up the gown.

I looked out through the double doors of the room and heard a remote splash. Through a hedge at the end of the lawn I could see specks of light blue. I walked out and followed the sound, rounding the hedge and ducking under a curling wisteria. He was there in the pool, gently swimming up and down. His head popped up out of the pool each time he drew breath, and each time he came up I got closer to realising where I had seen him before. He was the same thug who had attacked me in Mori's little caravan.

'Vespa,' I shouted.

He didn't hear me, but just kept on pulling himself towards the far end. I walked down there and stood waiting for him. Eventually, he got to the end of the pool, his knuckles holding on to the smooth, curving stone as he saw my feet. He looked up and seemed briefly confused. He pulled his hand down over his face to clear his eyes of water and looked at me again. Then he pulled himself out, his huge frame spilling water in all directions. He walked over to one of the white loungers and towelled himself off.

'You're the guy I met in Mori's dump, right?'

'Right.'

'What are you doing here?'

'Looking for you.'

'Did you follow me here from that shitty campsite?'

'No. I've been all over since then and the road leads back to you.'

'Does it?' He threw the towel down and looked at me. He had a barrel chest with grey hair. 'Drink?'

'Sure.'

'Basia,' he shouted impatiently. 'Basia.'

The woman came round the hedge and stared at him. There was animosity in the body language.

'Bring us drinks.'

She walked off towards a bamboo bar at the other end of the pool.

'Your wife?' I asked.

He sneered. 'My concubine. You know what they say about no Italians wanting to do the dirty jobs any more. Well, it's true. She's Bulgarian.'

'I thought you were surrounded by attractive young women.'

He stared at me, still sneering. 'Who told you that?'

'That's what I heard.'

'Sit down.' He jerked his chin towards a lounger. I sat on the edge, feeling precarious. 'What are you after?'

'I told you. I'm looking for a young girl who's gone missing.'

'What's it got to do with me?'

'You were looking for the man who's abducted her.'

'Still am,' he said.

'In the pool?'

He stared at me and then shouted furiously over to the woman in the short gown. 'Where are those drinks?'

She brought over two large glasses with straws. Vespa put his hand under her gown and grabbed one of her buttocks as she gave him his drink. She pulled his hand off, muttering to herself in a foreign language as she walked away.

'I'm still training her,' he said.

'You make her sound like an animal.'

'She is.' He nodded, smiling unpleasantly. 'So?'

I took a sip of the drink. It was a strong, fruity cocktail. I put it down and stared at Vespa. 'Let me tell you what I know and you tell me where I go wrong, OK?'

He assented with a twist of his head.

'Fabrizio Mori,' I said slowly, watching his reaction, 'is a blackmailer. He's spent his life gathering dirt so someone would pay him to bury it. There's enough dirt around that he's made a decent living in the past. He's found some more dirt and you're working for the man who is being blackmailed by Mori.'

Vespa threw his chin in the air to tell me to go on.

'I guess you're working for the TV magnate and now respectable politician, Di Angelo. He's the man you've always worked for, from what I hear. He's being blackmailed by Mori and he wants you to put a stop to it.'

He raised his eyebrows.

'What I don't understand,' I said, 'is what Simona Biondi's got to do with it.'

He looked at me, putting the straw of his drink in his mouth. He slurped deliberately loudly, as if defying me with his crude behaviour. Everything about him seemed vulgar. There was no veil cast over his lust, no disguise to his desires. But even that openness about his carnality seemed odd. It seemed like a front, only a pretence of honesty. It was the way he disguised something else.

'What exactly does studio manager mean?' I asked, losing patience with his insouciance.

'Studio manager? I'm like a talent scout. I find the flesh, the skirt.'

'All those showgirls who dance around but never speak?'

'Yeah, something like that. It ruins the illusion if you let them talk. It's fatal.' He smiled to himself.

'So you choose who goes on screen?'

He shook his head, smiling at my naivety. 'No, no. That was the boss's decision. Always his decision. He doesn't mind what programme we make, what the budget is, what the location is. None of that ever concerns him. But he always wants to choose the showgirls. His talent, he always says, is choosing the talent.'

'So you're like a pimp?'

Vespa looked at me and sneered. 'I introduce girls to him. That's all. What they do after that is between them.'

'But you serve them up to him, right?'

'Something like that. He used to want a different girl every night. That was my job. To make sure they're ready for him, as it were.'

'And his favourites go on screen?'

He raised his shoulders slowly. 'Some do, some don't.'

'What about Anna Sartori?'

'Who?' He had been towelling the back of his head, but suddenly stopped and looked at me.

'Anna Sartori. She was a girl who had been hustling with Mori back in the early nineties. Got about a bit and then wanted a slice of stardom. She went to see Gianni Esposito on one of Di Angelo's magazines, who sent her to you.'

'Yeah, Sartori,' he said, looking into the pool. 'She was a little temptress. I remember her all right.'

'So she came to see you and you sent her to Di Angelo?'

'She would have gone to one of his parties. He used to throw these parties for his advertisers. The girls were like the sweeteners, if you see what I mean.'

'At the Hotel del Fiume?'

He looked at me like he was surprised. 'Yeah, sometimes. They happened all over the place. How do you know about the del Fiume parties.'

'That's my job. I'm an investigator.'

He looked at me briefly, as if he had a second of respect.

'Sartori went missing. You remember that too?'

He went back to staring at the water, his round face catching the reflection of the sun and giving him shimmering glints on his skin.

'Yeah, I remember.'

He didn't say anything else. I watched his face but it was still, apart from those reflections dancing on his cheeks. He still had a thousand-yard stare, but whatever he was thinking, he seemed unlikely to share. We sat like that for a while, him staring at the water and me sucking on the straw of the cocktail.

'Does the name Simona Biondi mean anything to you?'

He rocked the top of his head like he was weighing up the price of his information.

'Mean anything?'

'There was a Biondi years ago. Way back when we were just starting out. Really cute piece.'

I thought of Simona's twitchy mother and struggled to imagine her as a beautiful girl. She didn't seem the type. 'When was this?'

'Same time as Sartori. Early nineties.'

'And you're sure this woman was called Biondi?'

'Sure. When you said you were looking for a girl called Biondi back at Mori's dump I immediately thought of her.'

'Why?'

'She dropped out of the game suddenly. Stopped showing up to parties. You know, she made me look bad so I called her. I wanted to know why she was flunking out.'

'Which was?'

'She didn't tell me. She just went off the radar. Some people did that. Just gave up on the whole circus.'

I thought about the dates in my head and it figured. I still struggled to imagine Simona's mother as a showgirl. She seemed too old, too fragile. And she had a career of her own anyway as a doctor. It was just about conceivable that she had been a showgirl, but I didn't really buy it. She must be in her mid-fifties now, meaning she was in her thirties back then, already a married woman and a mother. She was the wrong side of the hill as far as showbiz was concerned.

'You got a photo of her?'

He raised his eyebrows as if I were asking the impossible. 'I used to get hundreds of portfolios a week. Managers from all over the country sending me arty snaps of provincial girls in bikinis. They all looked the same after a while: all with their dim, desperate smiles, their coy way of being erotic and chaste at the same time. I chucked most of them in the bin.'

'And the ones you took on? Like Biondi?'

'I used to have to compile albums for the boss. He'd like to see snaps of them before getting them involved in his parties. Like I said, he chose them personally. "That one. Get me that one",' he growled. He bounced his index finger aggressively down onto the lounger, imitating his lecherous boss picking out girls like sweets in a shop.

'You still got those albums?'

'What difference does a photo make?'

'I want to check we're talking about the same person. Simona's mother hardly fits the description of...' I tried to remember what he had said, 'a cute piece.'

We downed the dregs of our cocktails and stood up. He pulled on a towelling bathrobe and waddled in front of me back towards the house. We went in through the double doors and up a wide stone staircase.

At the end of the corridor was a door leading into a narrow room. Vespa had to turn sideways to get past boxes on the floor. The shelves were all sagging under the weight of files. He turned and faced me, raising both his hands to the chaos all around. 'Good luck,' he said. 'I'm going to get some clothes on.' He squeezed past me and walked back down the corridor.

'Any filing system?' I shouted after him.

'The system's always been to throw things in and shut the door.' He disappeared into a bedroom.

I sat down on one of the cardboard boxes and looked at the chaos. There were shoeboxes and plastic pallets and box files. I peeked into the box nearest me and saw jiffy bags and A4 envelopes. I opened one of the envelopes and half a dozen shots of a girl in a bikini fell out. There was a covering letter from some talent agency in Naples. I went through them slowly, seeing more and more photos with varying degrees of eroticism: a girl lying on the beach as the waves lapped at her thighs, another eating an ice cream or emerging from a pool in a tight white T-shirt or cuddling a little kitten. They were all attractive but all strangely similar.

It took another half an hour before I found an album of photographs dated April 1992. I flicked through them but didn't find what I had been looking for. There were no snaps of Simona's twitchy mother. What there were, were intimate shots of Chiara, her sister: pictures of her reclining on a bed in underwear, her legs provocatively apart. There were other shots of her: ones of her backside, of her topless. They were the same sort of poses as all the others, but because I knew her, and liked her, it felt strange. She only looked seventeen or eighteen.

'This the girl?' I shouted down the corridor.

A door opened and Vespa walked out, still doing up his belt. 'Eh?'

'This the Biondi you're talking about?'

He took the folder from my hand and looked at it. 'That's her.' He nodded at a distant memory. 'That's the girl. Cute, huh? A lot of people liked her, that's why I was miffed when she quit.'

'And you never found out why she dropped out of the game?'

'Didn't try too hard to find out, to be honest. There's never been any shortage of girls wanting to get involved. Finding a replacement was like finding sand on the beach.'

'You ever wonder what happened to her?'

'I guessed.'

'And?'

'I just supposed she was pregnant. I never checked it out, but it was sort of an occupational hazard in their line.' He laughed nastily.

'Mind if I take this?'

He held out his palm to say I was welcome to it. We walked down the stairs together, him shouting for a drink as he straightened his hair with the flat of his hand. I left him there in the corridor, the little man commanding his domestic slave.

I drove back round to the Biondi pad and pulled up on the pavement outside their forbidding gate. I rang the intercom and they buzzed me in hurriedly. As soon as I got to the door, they pulled me inside, eager for information. The mother, Giovanna, had tried to disguise the alcohol on her breath with too much perfume and was fretting around me with questions. Her husband was impatient, almost swatting his wife away as he led me back into their living room.

'So?' he said.

'It seems that Simona is with a man.'

Giovanna sighed as if her daughter was already done for. 'A man,' she squawked.

'He's called Fabrizio Mori. Ever heard of him?'

They looked at each other briefly. It was the first time I had seen them exchange anything more than harsh words.

'You know him?' I asked.

'No, never heard of him,' Biondi said quickly. 'Who is he?'

His expression of ignorance was unconvincing, but I let it go.

'He's a hustler. I don't think they're romantically involved.'

'Then what does he want with her?'

'He seems set on making money.'

Giovanna put two palms to her cheeks and pressed them

against her face. She was guessing, I assumed, that I meant prostitution.

'Not that,' I said, looking at her. 'That's not part of his plan.'

'Where is he holding her?' Biondi asked angrily.

'I don't know. And he doesn't appear to be holding her as such. She's with him of her own volition.'

Biondi frowned, pulling his head backwards as if he didn't believe it.

'Witnesses I've spoken to seem to think he's not holding her against her will. They checked into a hotel a couple of nights ago. They had checked out by the time I got there.'

'A hotel,' the mother said, staring at the ceiling. She got up and walked towards the drinks cabinet, removing a glass stopper before pouring a generous shot of something. 'Drink?' She looked over to me.

'Sure.'

She brought me over a glass and I could see that her hands were shaking, making the ice rattle in her glass. I looked at her closely as she passed it to me: her skin looked pasty and her lipstick only made her seem somehow sadder, as if any brightness were put on.

'What do you know about this man she's with?' the father asked gruffly.

My hesitation gave the game away.

'What?' Biondi insisted.

'He's a photographer. Middle-aged.'

'Dangerous?'

'I don't think so. But certainly not the best company to keep.'

'Why not?'

I took a sip of the drink and wondered what to say. I looked up at Biondi and he was staring at me intently. 'He's done time for extortion,' I said quietly. 'He likes taking photos that embarrass people.'

'And he's taking snaps of Simona? Is that it?'

'I think she is the snap.'

'What does that mean?'

'I don't know.' I looked at both of them in case they could enlighten me, but they just stared back. 'I've got an idea that she is the evidence, or that she knows something about someone's wrong-doing. That's the only explanation I can come up with: that he's using her for another shake down.'

Biondi growled and looked at the floor. His wife's face looked thin and drawn as she stared at her empty tumbler.

'Did Simona need money?' I asked.

'Not at all. Why?'

'I'm only trying to understand why she would willingly go along with a man like Mori.'

They said nothing. We stood there like that in silence for a while. There was something heavy and tense about the silence, as though the couple's arguments were still echoing off the walls. I began to think that Mori might have been Simona's only ticket out of here and that she had taken a ride with him just to escape. Plenty of young girls go along with inappropriate older men just to break a bond with their parents. And there are plenty of older men around to help them make that break. I began to wonder whether it was just an unorthodox romance, a young girl's fling. Sometimes that's the only way an apparently perfect teenager can escape being perfect.

I walked towards the drinks trolley and put my glass back.

'Where are you going?' Biondi barked.

'To talk to Chiara.'

'Why? How can she help you? What's she got to do with this?' There was something in the way he said it that sounded wrong, like he knew how she could help me and wanted to know if I knew. It riled me. I was supposed to bring them anything I had, and yet it seemed as if they wouldn't give me anything back; as if they were holding out on me, not telling me the whole story.

'Information needs to travel both ways,' I said.

'What's that supposed to mean?'

'It means I need you to be more open with me, tell me more about Simona and her life.'

He put his palms out as if he would lay out everything on a plate. 'Anything you need to know, just ask. Anything.'

We stared at each other briefly and I sensed, instinctively, that he would have rather dropped the invisible plate than give it to me.

'I need to talk to Chiara,' I said.

'What on earth for?'

'She might be able to help.'

'I don't see how,' he said with the impatience of a man who was losing his grip on a lie.

'Is she here?'

'She's at home.'

'Where's that?'

He sighed as though it were a waste of time. 'It's just round the corner. It's number 67 on the street behind this one, the one that runs parallel to the main road out there.' He flicked his thumb at the heavy traffic outside.

I nodded, studying his face. I was still trying to work out

why a man who was apparently desperate to find his missing daughter would hold back information from the detective he had hired to find her. It didn't make sense. I guessed the search had led somewhere he didn't want it to go.

He must have picked up on my suspicion, because he became uncharacteristically friendly, putting a hand on my arm as we walked to the front door like we were old mates. It felt wrong and only made me more sure he was keeping something back.

I walked round the back of the Biondi villa to number 67 on the street behind. I found a buzzer with Biondi-Malaguzzi on it and held it down.

'Chi è?' asked an uncertain male voice.

'Castagnetti. I'm looking for Chiara.'

I heard him summon Chiara to the intercom. 'Sì?'

'Chiara? It's Castagnetti. The private detective hired by your parents.'

'Yes?'

'I need to talk to you.'

'Now?'

I told her it was important and she buzzed me in. 'Fifth floor,' she said.

I took the lift there and she was standing in the doorway in an apron. The smell of the evening's dinner was still in the air.

'Any news?'

'Some. Most of it unexpected.'

'Like?'

'Can we talk in private?'

She put her hands behind her back to untie the cords and pulled the apron over her head. She put it on a hook on the back of the kitchen door and introduced me to her husband, a tidy sort of man who had a dishcloth in his hand and was putting away the plates. She led me through a sitting room where two young boys were watching television and into a small office. Her fingers, nails varnished, held the door open for me, before shutting it behind us. It felt like an admission that there were secrets to spill.

She spun the office chair round and sat down, crossing her elegant legs. I sat in the red armchair opposite her.

'You used to work for Tony Vespa at the Di Angelo studios.'

Her face was rigid. 'I thought you were looking for Simona.'

'I am. And the search has led me here.'

'What do you mean?'

'Vespa tells me you quit working for him and for the studio. He told me you dropped out of the game.' I paused to let her finish the story, but the secret was so buried she seemed unable to say it.

She was staring at the bookshelf behind me, her head tilted back like she was scared of the way the past was rushing back towards her. She took deep breaths, her chest rising and falling as she sighed loudly.

'It was so long ago.' Her eyes were glazed over as if she were about to fall asleep. 'We didn't even understand what was going on.'

'We?'

'Anna and me.'

'Anna Sartori?'

'Right.'

'How did you know her?'

'She showed up here one day. Not here, at my parents. She was the daughter of a friend of my father's from the countryside.

96

She came to see us as she'd moved to Rome and didn't have many friends. We immediately became close. She was like the older sister I'd never had. She was wild, a real hell raiser, and I just got taken along for the ride.' She was still focused on one spot of the wall behind me and as she spoke she stared at it as if it were a window on the past. 'Anna and I would go out to parties that went on until midday the following day. The sort of parties where there was everything. Amazing food, a pool, endless drinks, any stimulants you needed, if you know what I mean. It was like everything was allowed. It was another world. I had only just left school. I don't think I had ever had more than a sip of wine in my life, and suddenly I was at these parties where people were . . .' She shook her head.

'What?'

She shrugged. 'When you're young, you think there are certain things you'll never do. But then you start making little compromises, giving in to tiny temptations, until you're doing all the things you thought you were going to avoid. The whole process is imperceptible. You just get used to being around rich, older men who are charming and generous. You get used to seeing people doing drugs, to going to parties where anything goes, you get used to being tipsy, to swimming naked with strangers, to being touched at sunrise when you're too tired or wired to object.'

She suddenly turned her gaze on me, like she was anticipating criticism. She still looked so young it was hard to think it must have been twenty years ago.

'I was so innocent, I barely understood what was happening. And then, when I understood it, I realised I just wasn't innocent any more. And you never get that back. It's gone for ever.'

She was talking in a kind of code, but it wasn't hard to read between the lines. 'I thought I was about to have it all that year, and instead I lost everything. I lost Anna, I lost myself.'

She blinked and tears fell onto her cheeks. She ignored them and kept talking, the pitch of her voice a little higher now. 'Anna was always being invited to parties. Every weekend there would be a different one.'

'Organised by who?'

'Usually the studio.'

'Di Angelo?'

'Right. We were even paid to go.'

'Paid?'

'We got an attendance fee from Vespa.'

'Why?'

'It was like an audition for being a showgirl, you had to dance for them, that sort of thing. We were like the chorus girls for the parties.' She shook her head, smiling bitterly at the memory. 'Anna was so desperate to make it on television she would have done anything.'

'And did she?'

Chiara looked at me sharply, as if determined to defend the memory of her missing friend. 'She had ambition, and she knew that the only way to get ahead was to play their game.'

'And what game was that?'

She rolled her eyes, impatient with my questions. 'Most of the people at these parties were advertisers. The kind of businessmen who bankrolled the studios by buying up airtime for their products. And they expected more than just an improvement in sales.'

'Meaning?'

'What do you think?' There was a bitter exasperation in her voice. 'We were there to service these cranky old men . . .' Her voice trailed off again.

It sounded like Tony Vespa really was some kind of pimp, supplying girls to dance and flirt and sleep with advertisers who were paying huge sums into the studio's coffers. The girls were so desperate to be on screen that they didn't seem to mind crawling under the covers to get there.

'Anna was so . . .' she paused, looking absently at the floor, 'so lost that she seemed ready to embrace anyone who could be a father to her. She didn't just go upstairs at those parties because she was ambitious. I think she really needed to be embraced by an older man. It was the classic case of a young girl who looked for her father in other men. But they only wanted her body briefly and each time she was abandoned again she looked more desperately for someone who would really love her.' She sighed heavily. 'The tragedy is that she did meet someone who loved her and, just as she seemed about to find happiness, she disappeared.'

'Who was that?'

'Oh, some guy who had a yogurt empire,' she laughed at how ridiculous it sounded. 'He was one of the regular advertisers on the prime-time slots. They got really close for a while. She became his mistress, you know a fixed item, and he lobbied hard for her to get a run-out on screen. For a while, it looked like it was all going to work out for her, but then it just . . .' she shrugged, 'it just went wrong.'

'You mean she went missing?'

Chiara nodded. 'She was so close to everything she longed for. She had an older man who loved her. She was about to become a chorus girl on TV. And then...' She raised her hands, throwing them in the air like a slow-motion explosion. 'That was it. She was gone.'

I looked at her briefly. Her chest was shaking as her breathing became staccato.

'You said,' I spoke quietly, 'that you lost yourself as well that year.'

She growled softly and reached for a packet of tissues on the desk behind her. 'I was introduced to someone by Vespa. I had no idea who he was, but you could tell by the way Vespa was behaving that he was some big cheese.'

'You remember his name?'

'Hard to forget. Giorgio Gregori. Vespa told me it would be a big step in my career if I was good to him. That was always the phrase he used. "Be good to him".'

'Were you?'

She shut her eyes and her head rocked back as she exhaled in derision. 'Good's not the word. All I could think about was getting ahead. There were all these girls at these parties, all wanting the same thing: to make it on TV. This Gregori told me he could have a word with Di Angelo, said it would be real easy to get me on screen. We had a meal and lots to drink and then went back to his place. I knew what was coming but I was still shocked by it.' She was whispering now. 'He sat in an armchair and just gave me orders. Started insulting me, telling me I was a whore, that I was a dirty slut who needed to be straightened out. And I was,' she looked at me now with an apologetic smile. 'I knew I was being paid for this, that Vespa would be giving me a big envelope of cash when I got back to the studios. So I let him do what he wanted to me. He would pull my hair to get me where he wanted. He would slap me for being dirty, for doing what he wanted. He liked me to protest, so that he could hit me harder.'

'Sounds like a nice guy.'

'He was a piece of shit. A true piece of shit. Each time there were little variations, but it was usually the same stuff. He would start by telling me how he only needed to make one call and Di Angelo would put me up there on the stage with the other stars. He would be almost romantic, like he cared about my future. Then we would get to some hotel or flat and he would flip. It was like he was possessed, like he had to blame me for something. He was wild, nasty. And afterwards he wouldn't even want to talk. He would just tell me to get out, like that was it. Like he was ashamed about what had happened. And I would get paid by Vespa and try to forget about it until the next time. You do something once,' she said in a dreamy voice, 'and get paid for it and you think you'll never do it again. But then you do, because you need the money or the advancement. And then it becomes a habit and you lie to yourself about what you do or what you've become.' She looked at me with tired eyes and nodded. 'You must think I'm terrible.'

I shook my head. I had seen much worse than an ambitious girl using her charms to get ahead. I looked at her and she was shaking her head now, like she either didn't believe me or couldn't believe what her former self had done.

'That's why I say I lost myself.'

'And you lost Simona too?'

She looked at me sharply. 'What do you mean?'

I didn't say anything else, but watched her face. I had a hunch about something now and probably only Chiara could tell me if I was right or not. I guessed that she had dropped out of the game because she had fallen pregnant. And that the child she was carrying was Giorgio Gregori's. Her parents had adopted the child, pretending to everyone that the two girls in their household were sisters. It meant that Chiara's reputation stayed undamaged. And if Simona was the result of the tawdry liaison between Chiara and Gregori, she would be living proof that Di Angelo used to serve up young girls to oil the wheels of his business empire.

Chiara was breathing heavily now, moving as if pained by something physically coming to the surface. She almost looked like she was going to be sick. She made a couple of false starts, clamping her mouth shut just as something was about to come out. Then she shut her eyes and took some deep breaths.

'My parents found out I was pregnant. There's only so long you can hide something like that. They decided everything before I even knew what was going on. They were going to bring up Simona as their own daughter. I didn't want her anyway. I thought she would be a constant reminder of that man. Of what I had done. I was fine with it. She was supposed to be my little sister and that was OK. But then, when she was born,' her voice suddenly went up an octave, 'she was this helpless, tiny baby. My baby.

'People always used to say how close we were, despite the age difference, and I used to think that they knew, that they must have known. But no one ever did. They just thought we were sisters. We've always been so close. I've tried to be like a mother to her, even though I've done everything to disguise it.' She had given up keeping the tears back now. 'Sometimes I've just wanted to hug her, you know, to hold her and tell her the truth, but I couldn't. Not once I'd lied about it all those years, it was impossible. And by now she's been my sister so long that it seems almost true.'

'And not even Simona knows the truth?'

She shook her head.

'And your husband?'

She was still shaking her head, moving her chin from side to side as though it were a slow, heavy pendulum.

I leant forward and touched her shoulder as it bounced with her sobs. I watched her lap being darkened with her tears.

There was an abrupt knock at the door and her husband came in. He looked at us for a second. 'Everything OK?'

She wiped away a tear with the back of her hand and nodded. 'Fine.' She looked at him and smiled apologetically. 'It's fine.'

I took my hand off her shoulder, not wanting to appear intimate in front of her husband.

'OK,' he said, unconvinced, and shut the door again.

We heard his footsteps retreating down the corridor. 'I don't know how I'll ever tell him all this,' she whispered. 'Or what I'll tell the boys.'

'The most important thing right now is to find Simona.'

She looked at me with longing. There was something attractive about her damp lips as she smiled wistfully. 'I should have told you all this at the beginning.'

I shrugged as if it didn't matter. 'Tell me about Giorgio Gregori.'

She sighed, throwing her head back to look at the ceiling. 'I only found out afterwards who he was.'

'Go on.'

'The head of Teleshare Italia.'

'What's that?'

'It's the organisation that measures viewing figures.' She rested her head on her shoulder as she moved her eyes from the ceiling to me. 'Get it?'

'Di Angelo's studio was providing...' I tried to be tactful, 'entertainment for the head of Teleshare?'

'Right.' Her faraway stare had returned. Her gaze was fixed on the wall behind my shoulders. 'And Simona,' she said quietly, almost to herself, 'is the living evidence of that, of that entertainment.'

I felt like I finally understood Mori's interest in the young girl. She was the proof that Di Angelo's TV station was crooked, that it had been employing high-class call girls to service the men who controlled the revenue streams. Not just the important advertisers, but the quango that measured viewing figures. Increases of even fractions of a per cent in audience share could mean millions more in advertising revenue for a studio. With tens or hundreds of thousands of extra viewers, a station could increase its charges to advertisers. Giorgio Gregori, the head of Teleshare, was like the fairy godfather, the man who – with a wave of his wand – could give a media magnate pots of gold. So the media magnate had sent round young girls to please the fairy godfather to persuade him to nudge up the viewing figures. Mori, I guessed, knew what had gone on and was using Simona to squeeze some money out of Gregori or, more probably, Di Angelo.

'How did Mori know about it?' I asked her.

She shrugged.

'You never told him?'

'I hardly knew him. I only met him once or twice.'

'With Anna?'

'Right. They were friends, sort of. I knew he had hung out with Anna in the past. They were from the same tiny village somewhere in Le Marche.'

'Where was that?'

She shrugged again. 'I can't remember, but they were from the same village, or certainly the same area.'

'What was he like?'

'A charlatan. I don't know what she saw in him. He had nothing going for him except her.'

'And now Simona.'

'Yeah, that's what he was like. He used people, nothing more. Are you sure it's him?'

'Seems that way.' I pulled out the old photograph of Mori that his brother had given me. 'This is him, right?' I passed it over and she looked at it, shaking her head in disbelief that he was back in her life.

'Yeah, that's him.' She turned the photograph over to look at the back, and then looked at the shot again. 'Anna must have told him about me before she went missing. I told her I was pregnant. She was more or less the only one I told.'

'And she knew who the father was?'

'Sure. She knew.'

Chiara and I looked at each other, thinking the same thing. That Mori must have known about Simona's existence for years. But it was only when her photograph appeared in a magazine recently that he knew where to look for her, where to find her outside her family home. And it was only now, now that Di Angelo was a senator in parliament pontificating about the state of the nation, that he might be prepared to pay big money to keep his skeletons in the cupboard.

'Where does this Gregori live?' I asked.

'Gregori?'

'Sure.'

She shut her eyes. 'He used to be in Via Napoli. One of the apartments on the right of that courtyard opposite the fountain.'

I stood up to go. I looked at her, unsure of what to say. She just sat there, staring ahead. I put a hand on her shoulder briefly and walked out.

Her husband was watching television with his sons. I nodded in his direction and he came over to let me out.

'She's been really shaken by this whole Simona thing,' he said, as if explaining his wife's tears.

'I think everyone's been shaken by it.'

'Any news?'

I shook my head. 'Old news. There's stuff that happened a long time ago. I think it's bringing back bad memories.'

'What do you mean?' He had an uneven smile, and I wondered how much, deep down, he actually knew or suspected.

'Secrets are like fireworks,' I said. 'You don't see them until they explode.'

He looked at me quizzically as we shook hands. I got in the lift and looked at my reflection in the mirror. I hadn't shaved for five days and there was a purple patch above my eye where Vespa had hit me in Mori's caravan. I looked like a boozer after a bar brawl.

I went and sat in the car and watched the world. Pedestrians kept walking past with rectangular shopping bags with string handles. The shops' logos were printed on the outside. I was tired and bemused. Bemused that the world kept on shopping whatever the warnings, as if it were vital to be well dressed for the economic apocalypse. Bemused that people could keep going despite the grief and terror and tragedy all around them. And bemused that parents who were desperate to find their only daughter seemed to be holding out on me. It didn't make sense.

I found Via Napoli and Gregori's place easily enough. It was one of those old palazzi that made Rome seem timeless. I walked in through the main archway and found an old staircase to the right. The centres of the stone steps were worn with time and the stone bannisters had been polished by centuries of palms.

At the top of the staircase there was an internal balcony. I walked along it, looking at the dark wooden doors with their oval brass nameplates. The whole place felt old and august.

At the end of the line I saw the name Gregori on a plaque. I stared at it for a second, not sure what to expect. I realised I didn't know if he was married, if he had family, if he had other children.

I rang the bell. Almost a minute later the door opened and an elderly woman stood in the doorway. She was wearing an apron and wiping her hands on a blue towel.

'Hello.'

'I'm looking for Giorgio Gregori.'

'And you are?'

'Castagnetti. I'm a private detective.'

'My brother's very frail. He's not really up to seeing visitors.'

'A young girl's life is in danger.'

She frowned, looking at me as if she suspected it was some kind of wind-up. 'What girl?'

'Can I come in?'

She held the door open, looking at me as I moved past her and into the hallway. It was the kind of place that was furnished entirely with antiques. There were large oil paintings with curling gold-leaf frames, scratched mirrors above marble mantlepieces, an oak table with a row of reclining, embossed invitations.

'This was my parents' house,' the woman said. 'Giorgio has lived here ever since they passed away in the 1970s. I've been looking after him since he fell ill.'

'And you're his sister?'

'Mariangela Gregori,' she held out a hand. 'Who is this girl who is missing? I'm sure Giorgio can't help you. He's barely left his bedroom for the last year.'

I stared at her kind face, wondering how much she knew about her brother.

'Coffee?'

We went into the kitchen and she went through the habitual motions: water, granules, heat. She asked me a couple of courteous questions as we waited for it to bubble up to the top chamber. When it hissed its arrival, she poured it out and led me through to a dining room. We sat on the corner of a huge, rectangular table surrounded by cabinets of silver bowls and decorated dishes.

'My brother hasn't got long,' she said.

'I won't need long,' I said.

'I mean, he won't be with us much longer. He was diagnosed with emphysema years ago and is slowly going downhill.'

'I'm sorry.'

'He's always been so active, so strong. It's strange to see him lying there all day, barely able to feed himself.'

'He had a very successful career,' I said vaguely.

She nodded. 'He did. He was always being asked to chair this or that. People knew he was reliable.'

I smiled at the irony. Reliability was what got you work in this country. You had to do what you were told, making little compromises all the way to the top until, if you got there yourself, you had made so many compromises that you had to start forcing other people to make them to cover up your tracks.

'Didn't he work for Teleshare a long time ago?' I asked innocently.

'He set it up,' she said. 'Before then, there was no trustworthy measure of public taste. He was the first to devise a system to measure audience figures scientifically.'

She was clearly the sort of sister who idolised her older brother. I didn't want to burst her bubble, but I was facing a race against time to find Simona.

'The girl I'm looking for is his daughter,' I said abruptly.

She put down her cup and laughed. 'I'm sorry,' she shook her head, 'Giorgio doesn't have a daughter.'

'I believe he does. I need to talk to him.'

She stared at me, still trying to work out if I was serious. I took out my photograph of Simona and passed it across the polished table. 'This is the girl.'

'He doesn't have a daughter,' she frowned, still sceptical.

'I don't think he knows he has one. I need to talk to him. He deserves to know.'

'You're sure about this?'

I nodded. She picked up the snap of Simona again and looked at it, staring at the face with a confused smile. When she turned her gaze on me she looked changed, like something had been lit inside her.

'She's very beautiful.'

'So is her mother.'

'Who is she?'

'I would rather talk to your brother. Your niece,' I leant on the word so that she listened, 'could be in danger.'

She got up and went down a corridor. I heard her knock gently on a door. As it opened, I could hear the old man coughing repeatedly, groaning as he failed to dislodge the obstructions in his lungs.

A few minutes later she came back. 'He's weak but he's still cantankerous.' She smiled apologetically.

We walked down the corridor together and again she gave a deferential knock before going in.

'This is the gentleman,' she said, motioning towards me.

I looked at the double bed where Gregori was propped upright. He was thin and drawn. His face was grey and his lower lip was wobbling like he couldn't control it. He was wearing pyjamas that looked like a pinstripe suit. He was an invalid but he still meant business. His eyes were stern, staring at me as though he would give no quarter.

'All right,' he said abruptly to his sister, nodding her out of the room. 'What's this about?' He looked at me through wiry eyebrows.

There was nowhere to sit, so I stood at the corner of his bed.

'A young girl's gone missing,' I said. 'She's only eighteen. I've been hired by her family to find her.'

He was still staring at me, his jaw juddering involuntarily. 'And?'

'I need your help.'

He started coughing, his whole, frail body folding as he tried to clear his throat. I watched him and waited for him to finish. He spat into a blue handkerchief. I took out the snap of Simona and passed it over. He looked up at me before snatching it from me in his thin, grey fingers. He stared at the page from the magazine. There was no emotion on his face. He passed it back to me with a nonplussed shrug.

'Never seen her,' he said. 'I've been in this cursed bed for months. I can't help you.' He stared at the far wall as if the interview were ended. But then he started coughing again.

'Can I get you some water?' I asked.

He seemed irritated and shook his head. 'Cigarettes were a weakness of mine. And we all pay for our weaknesses in the end.'

'I heard you had another weakness. You might be about to pay for that too.'

'What are you talking about?'

'Young girls.'

He sneered. 'You think I'm responsible for the disappearance of that girl?'

'I think you're responsible for her appearance.'

He frowned, like he couldn't follow. 'I've never been married. I had little histories with women. Little romances now and again.'

'Not much romance from what I heard.'

'What are you talking about?'

'I heard that Tony Vespa used to send you girls. Why would he do that?'

'No one ever sent me girls. They came to me.' He tried to push himself upright with a weak arm. 'I've always been fortunate with women.' He said it like there was still a chance he would be again.

I offered him my most derisive smile. 'They were sent. They were call girls. Why would Vespa pick up your brothel bill?'

'I've never heard of this Vespa,' he said dismissively.

'Di Angelo?'

'He runs a TV studio. I was in the industry. We knew each other. So?'

'And his studio used to send girls your way.'

'I told you, I've never paid for a woman in my life.'

'Right. Someone else picked up the bill. This girl,' I held up the snap again, 'she's your daughter.'

Nothing changed. He still stared at me as his chin bounced up and down. I waited for him to say something, to show some disbelief or curiosity, but he just stared at me.

'The mother of this girl is one of the escorts Vespa used to send your way. Her name was Chiara Biondi.'

He smiled like he wanted to show he was still smart. 'Bull.'

I passed the snap over again. 'Your daughter,' I said. 'You got any other kids?'

'I haven't got any kids.'

'Then she's your only child. By the looks of you, you'll be heading into eternity pretty soon. But she,' I pointed at the photo, 'she might get there before you if you don't help me. She's eighteen, an innocent young girl. She's your daughter and you can save her if you answer a couple of questions.'

He was staring at the photo differently now. Staring at it longingly as if it was his last hope of happiness, as if there was something left that might complete his life before he checked out.

'She's been abducted,' I said quietly, 'by a petty crook who likes to squeeze cash out of people with secrets to hide. My guess is he's headed either here or, more likely, to Di Angelo.'

'Why?'

'Because she's the living evidence of what went on back in the nineties.'

His eyes were glazed over, like he was trying to remember.

'Di Angelo's in politics now,' I reminded him. 'He's gone clean, or pretended to. My guess is that he would rather lose the girl than his career.'

Gregori was still looking at the photograph.

'That's your daughter. She's in danger. Don't you want to meet her before you die?' He was still staring at the photograph with a look of incomprehension. 'Why don't you tell me what went on?'

He didn't say anything. I could hear the soporific tick-tock of an old grandfather clock in the corner. His breathing was slow now, like he was preparing a final confession.

'I know what it looks like to you,' he said slowly, fixing me with his yellowy eyes. 'You use words like corruption and call girl. Words that make me sound like some sort of gangster.' He drew breath noisily. 'It was never like that.'

'Tell me what it was like.'

He pushed his head back into the pillow and looked at the ceiling. 'In the late eighties there were hundreds of private TV stations.' His voice was almost a whisper and I had to lean close to hear properly. 'Every local businessman wanted his own channel. It didn't take much. All you needed was a room, a girl with a nice smile and a big bosom, and a cameraman. Everyone was trying it. The only problem was that they needed income, and the only way to get that was advertising. And no advertisers would buy space if they didn't know how many eyeballs were watching their ad. With a newspaper you know, more or less, your readership. You know how many copies you've sold. But advertisers felt that television was just sending images up into the dark sky and they had no idea which households were picking them up. The private TV stations needed advertisers and advertisers needed to know viewing figures.'

'So?'

'I set up a company to suit them both. It measured the viewing figures in order that the stations could present clear data, and advertisers could evaluate whether it was worth buying advertising space on any of these channels.'

'How?'

He rolled his head on the pillow and looked at me. 'How what? How did we measure it? We gave a couple of hundred households little set-top boxes that measured their viewing habits. We amplified that sample to get an idea of national viewing. It gave us, and the advertisers, an accurate reflection of what programmes were popular and what not.'

'Accurate?'

'It was an estimate of course. We were merely elaborating a sample, so there's always a margin of error. But it was clearer than anything they had had in the past.' Something caught in his throat and he started rasping. He pushed himself up on his elbows and spat into the handkerchief again. 'The advertisers wanted accuracy and were always lobbying me to expand the sample. If you have a few hundred households as a sample, the margin of error is fairly high, but if you have a few thousand, it's greatly reduced. I explained that there were cost implications. Back in the late eighties those set-top boxes cost hundreds of thousands of lire. But we slowly amplified the sample.'

'And made it more accurate?'

He stared at the ceiling and smiled slightly. 'Accurate.' He said it dismissively. 'What's accurate? We certainly let the advertisers know exactly what our sample was watching.'

'But?'

'What has any of this got to do with this missing girl?' He still had the photograph between his fingers.

'Why wasn't it accurate?'

His breathing sounded laboured. Each time his chest rose it gurgled like static on an old radio. 'We fudged,' he said softly, 'the sample. Our staff were spending hours going through the demographics, trying to find the right balance within our sample. You know,' he coughed, 'an old woman, a young woman, a rich man, a poor man. All that stuff. It was taking months and months to get a balanced sample, and even then there was no knowing whether it was really balanced.' He paused, looking again at the ceiling. I followed his gaze and saw the yellow stains of nicotine. 'Di Angelo came to me saying they had done some market research years ago and had all sorts of demographics that might save us time.'

'He had his own, prepared sample of people?'

He nodded. 'He was suggesting who we should involve. It saved us time and I had no reason to doubt the market research. At least, not until the figures started coming in. As soon as the enlarged sample was up and running, Di Angelo's studios were recording magnificent ratings. Stuff he could only have dreamt of a few weeks or months before.'

'You had given these set-top boxes to his best friends?'

'Something like that. They must have left their TVs on his station all day and all night. Back then he was only a small player, one of hundreds of aspiring media players. He struggled to get to one per cent most of the time. And suddenly he was recording two, three, four per cent. Across the nation. At night it got close to double figures. Crazy results.'

'So you were accurately recording what people were watching. It's just that the people you were gathering data from were Di Angelo plants?'

'Some of them. I was very uncomfortable. I arranged a meeting with him and he admitted it all. He shrugged his shoulders and said sorry, said he had had to do it to build his business. I was astonished at how up front he was about his dishonesty. That was what really struck me. Never denied it. I complained that he had damaged my reputation, that I was compromised, but he was convinced no one would ever know. He said we were now allies,' he paused to catch his breath, 'which meant I was in his large pocket.'

Gregori was shaking his head on the pillow, moving his hairy ears from one side to the other. 'He was all charm, said he was desperate to make it up to me. He offered me money. A lot of money. I said that would only compromise me further.'

'So?'

'I walked out. I felt my career was over. Someone would find out about it. I was supposed to be some sort of referee but I had been bought by one of the players. I wanted to go public, to say what had happened.' He sighed heavily.

'But you didn't.'

He looked at me, sensing my disapproval.

'And then one evening I was sitting here on my own. I had just got back from dinner somewhere. The doorbell went and there was a young woman standing there.' He closed his eyes and frowned slightly. 'She was very young and beautiful. She asked if she could come in, asked if there was anything she could do. Said it in such a way that didn't leave much doubt about what was on offer.'

'And you knew she was sent by Di Angelo?'

'I didn't ask and frankly I didn't care at that point. I took her in, gave her a drink.' He rolled his head to look at me again. 'I thought it would never happen again.'

'But?'

'It just went on. I never even spoke to Di Angelo, but girls would come round here, or I would get invited to parties that were unlike anything I had ever seen before. Wild, extraordinary parties. There were Cubans, Brazilians, Russians, the lot. I became,' he closed his eyes, 'someone different. I was cruel with them. I felt like I owned them.'

'Whereas it was Di Angelo that owned you?'

He gave a tired nod. 'As the company got bigger, we kept increasing the sample. And each time someone from his station would subtly suggest the precise people that should be included. I just went along with it.'

'And his viewing figures kept rising?'

'Of course. Double figures by then were normal. In terms of percentages, he was in the teens and twenties. This was a man who had been delivering freesheets door to door only ten years earlier. And now he was charging advertisers billions and billions of lire per minute of airtime. He had found the perfect formula to print money. And more than that, he was always surrounded by hundreds of young women who were desperate to get on screen and who were prepared to do anything to get there.'

'And Chiara Biondi was one of those girls who was sent your way?'

He nodded. 'Chiara. That's right.'

We sat like that for a minute. The whole thing was clear now. Chiara Biondi was one of the young girls who had kept Gregori sweet. He was sent girls in return for bumping up Di Angelo's viewing figures. No one had ever known about it. And now Di Angelo had reinvented himself as a politician, the sort of red-blooded man that the parliament of a red-blooded country needed. He had presented himself as an honest Joe, the sort of straight-talking businessman who would clean up the corrupt habits of politics. But this was the kind of scandal that could blast a big hole in his new career. Mori, the paparazzo, knew about the story from Anna Sartori, and when he saw Simona's photo in the magazine he knew he had living evidence of the deal between Di Angelo and Gregori's Teleshare. She was the walking proof that Di Angelo had made millions from being a high-end pimp.

'How do I know she's mine?' Gregori asked.

'They can test for these things now.'

'There might not be time for that.' He looked around his dishevelled bed as if to say that he was on the home straight.

'You could take her mother's word for it.'

'I don't know what that's worth.'

'I do. And, with respect, she really didn't want her daughter to be yours.'

'That so?' He closed his eyes briefly. 'I haven't always been a good man. I've made a lot of mistakes in my life. I've only realised how many since I've been immobilised here in bed. Death focuses the mind that way. That period was an aberration, a time when I was prepared to play his game to get the rewards. I didn't know how dirty the game was, or how fleeting those rewards.'

'Something good might have come out of it,' I said, wanting to nudge him back towards Simona.

'Will you bring her here?' he said.

'Simona?' I looked at him, surprised by his apparent sentimentality.

He nodded. 'My one regret in life is not having any children. And now I'm confined to this bed you come and tell me I have a daughter. I might be in a position to make amends for what I've done.'

'Not if she doesn't make it.'

'You really think she's in danger?'

'Sure. I need your help.'

'There's nothing I can do. Look at me.'

'I need you to make a phone call. Call Di Angelo, tell him to meet me.'

He was frowning now, weighing up the chances, I guessed, of even getting through to the senator. His chest rose slowly, sounding like a draining plughole. He was breathing heavily, as if our conversation had exhausted him. I looked around the room as I listened to his wheezy breaths. There were small pots of pills lined up on his bedside table. On the opposite wall the curtains were being gently sucked out of the window by the wind.

'Pass me that phone.' He pointed at a cordless standing up-right in its cradle. He gave orders like he was used to being obeyed. 'And that book.'

I handed them both over and he groaned as he fingered through the leather book, looking for a number. He dialled like an old man, using his index finger instead of his thumb as he held the handset at arm's length to see the numbers. He listened, then hung up again.

'"Non-existent number" it said. I'll try another.'

He dialled again and this time I heard the phone ringing the other end. A woman's voice answered.

'I need to speak to Di Angelo,' he said abruptly. 'It's Giorgio Gregori.'

Something was said and he was put on hold. Eventually, he was asked to leave a message.

'Tell him,' he shut his eyes as if it would add emphasis to his words, 'tell him Giorgio Gregori called. It's very important that he allows . . .' he put his hand over the mouthpiece, 'what's your name?'

'Castagnetti.'

'. . . that he allows a private investigator called Castagnetti to see him. It's urgent. It's my dying wish,' he said melodramatically.

He hung up and looked at me. 'It used to be that he would call me every day. Now he's gone so high up in the world, he wouldn't even take calls from his mother.'

'What was he like back then?'

'Di Angelo?' He smiled. 'He was like a boy, a young boy who wanted to be loved by everyone. He was a back-slapping sort, always trying to make friends, telling jokes, oiling the wheels. He was absurdly generous, giving presents to everyone and to their wives and their mistresses. If someone was in hospital, he would send a huge bouquet of flowers. He was constantly trying to make a gesture, a gift, a statement, that marked him out as some sort of benevolent patron.'

Gregori coughed again, turning away from me as he produced more phlegm.

'He was from Naples and had charm and cunning in equal measure. When he wanted something from you, he would beg and plead and weep. He really was like a little boy who was trying to get sweets from his parents. He could charm the birds from the trees.'

'And if he didn't get his own way?'

Gregori shook his head. 'He always did.'

'Surely not always?'

'Anything that stood in his way was simply bought. Around the time I knew him, Di Angelo was so rich he could buy anything and anyone. Of course, people didn't think they were being bought. They were offered a place on the board of this or that. Usually with a salary of millions of lire for three afternoons a year. They were offered a job, or their own show.'

'Or a girl?'

He looked at me sharply. 'Sure. That's just the way it worked. There didn't seem to be any harm in it. It was business.'

'And pleasure.'

'The two were never separated in Di Angelo's world. He made money out of his passion, and got plenty of passion for his money.'

'So why did he go into politics? He wasn't passionate about that.'

'You'd have to ask him. My guess is that it was necessary to defend his business interests. He saw the whole political order of the First Republic collapsing and imploding, and was spooked. There were fanatics and puritans on the loose, and a few of them had been muttering about breaking up his media monopoly. By then he had a publishing house, a few newspapers, a stable of magazines and the most-watched channel on the peninsula. If he hadn't gone into politics it might have all been taken away, broken up and sold off.'

He was talking more and more. He seemed eager to explain to me the way things worked, like I was a naïve youth with no idea of the real world.

'Before him, politics had been grey, full of dour, pompous politicians and the genteel corruption of eloquent gentlemen. Di Angelo came along and wanted a parliament more like a TV studio: colourful, noisy, full of dreams and aspiration and beautiful young women. If he'd had his own way, he would have hung a glitter ball from the ceiling. When he came along, the shrewd remnants of the First Republic joined his revolution because they knew it was a reactionary movement, an attempt to change everything and so keep it just the same. Those old politicians were scathing about Di Angelo's lack of class, his want of finesse, but they knew he was the director of the tragic opera now and they still wanted a role, however small. Catholic voters saw Di Angelo's veneer of piety, and solidly far-right opinions, as far preferable to the real piety, and mildly left-wing tendencies, of the opposition. He couldn't lose. He never does.'

'And how will he react if a hustler from the past starts digging up the dirt from decades ago?'

Gregori stared at the wall opposite and narrowed his eyes. 'My guess is that he'll laugh it off. He might not even understand what he's done wrong, what he's being accused of. And if he does, he'll simply offer the man a large sum of money and be done with it.'

'Nothing more drastic?'

He laughed. 'More drastic?'

'You heard about a girl called Anna Sartori?'

Gregori frowned, as if the name rang a distant bell.

'She went missing years ago. She had been at the fringe of the Di Angelo empire. She's never been seen since. I'm worried the same might happen to my clients' daughter.'

'Don't be silly. Di Angelo's a fool, not a gangster. He's a businessman. He entices and charms. He's in public life anyway.' He shook his head, like my suggestion was preposterous. 'Bring her here when you find her.'

'Simona? When I find her I'm taking her back to her parents.'

He tried to turn over to face me, but only managed to raise his far shoulder slightly. 'I'm her father.'

'Some father.'

He stared at me with anger in his rheumy eyes. I got up to leave and his thin fingers reached around my sleeve. 'Bring her here. Please.'

'I'll bring her if she wants to come.'

He nodded and slowly let go of my sleeve. I got up and opened the door. His sister was standing in the corridor, pretending to sweep. We looked at each other as the old man shouted after me, repeating that he demanded to see his own daughter. She went in to calm him down and I let myself out.

Di Angelo lived in a large palazzo that made up the entirety of one side of a block. There was an archway off the main road with two armed guards outside. They stood in little sentry boxes wearing sunglasses and earpieces. They were looking left and right, more to check for girls, I thought, than for trouble. I saw them shout at each other as an attractive girl walked towards them. They said something to her as she passed but she ignored them. I was about to ask the one on the right how to get in when he thumbed at a glass box inside the arch. I moved between the guards and knocked on the window of the booth. Inside, a man was sitting in front of a dozen monitors, all showing images of gateways and doors. He pulled up the window.

'Good afternoon,' he said formally.

'I'm here to see Di Angelo.'

He looked at me, moving his head back slightly as if he didn't think I had a chance. 'You got an appointment?'

'No, but he's expecting me. My name's Castagnetti; I'm a private investigator.'

'That so? Hang on.' He pulled the window down again and picked up a phone. I couldn't hear what he was saying, but he looked back towards me like he had been asked to give a description. He nodded, listening to someone the other end, then nodded again. He hung up and pushed up the window.

'The senator's not in residence,' he said grandly, like he was talking about a monarch.

'Do you know when he'll be back?'

He shook his head.

'Can't I wait for him inside?'

'I'm afraid not.'

'Tell them it's an emergency. A young girl has been abducted.'

He smiled condescendingly, like I was another of the loons he saw all the time. 'I'm sorry,' he said, pulling down the window and turning back to his monitors.

In front of me the two huge doors that filled the archway were studded with blunt metal points. Inside those two doors was a wicket gate for pedestrians.

'I'll wait,' I said, knocking on the glass of the booth. He didn't turn round or acknowledge me.

I went back past the guards and onto the other side of the street. It was a wide boulevard with palm trees every ten metres or so. Their flopping leaves looked like the tops of pineapples. Traffic came in bursts as lights went green then red: a surge of hot, noisy metal, then nothing for thirty seconds, then another surge. I watched the entrance to Di Angelo's building, seeing no one go in and no one come out. The guards continued to shout at the occasional woman walking past.

Eventually, after almost two hours, an Audi with blackened windows approached the archway, preceded by two motorcycle outriders. The large gate opened and the motorcycles let the car go in first. As the gates opened I could see inside to a large courtyard: there was a fountain in the centre, water flowing off the circular stand below to create a thin curtain of water that glinted in the sun. There were other expensive cars in the courtyard and, just as the gates began to close, I saw the driver leap out of the car and open the back passenger-side door. A stocky man in a double-breasted suit got out.

I crossed the road and went back to the booth. I knocked hard on the glass.

'Will he see me now?'

The glass went up again. 'You still here?'

'I told you, it's an emergency. I was told Di Angelo would see me.'

'By whom exactly.'

'Giorgio Gregori.'

'Never heard of him.'

'Your boss has.'

'That so?' He looked at me scornfully again, and slowly picked up the phone. He made it very clear how reluctant he was to bother the people inside on my behalf. The glass came down again. He hung up, stood up, and came out under the archway himself with a lollipop-shaped piece of plastic.

'You know the routine. Arms up, legs apart.'

I stood in star position as he ran the thing all over my limbs. Coins and keys set the thing beeping and he handed over a tray.

'In there.'

He did the routine again and this time it was quiet. He handed me back the tray and I took my stuff. He pulled out his own keys and opened the pedestrian door.

'Go up the staircase directly in front of you.'

I walked towards the staircase of wide stone steps. As I reached the bottom step I could hear the click of heels coming down from the flight above. A woman in a knee-length blue skirt and tight white shirt held out her hand towards me.

'You're Mr Castagnetti? Pleasure. I'm Rosanna Bianchi, one of Mr Di Angelo's secretaries.'

'How many's he got?'

She smiled. 'A few.'

We walked up the staircase side by side and she led me into a large waiting room. There were fraying armchairs around the walls and paintings between the huge windows. The room echoed to the sound of quickstep secretaries rushing to and fro as they made arrangements on the phone. The woman showed me to one of the armchairs and told me Di Angelo would see me when he was free. I waited over an hour.

'He'll see you now,' she said eventually, standing by the door.

I walked over and she led me down the corridor into an end room that was dark. The shutters were pulled down and the only natural light was from the thin, horizontal lines between the slats. There was a lamp in a corner with a large green shade. Underneath it, in an armchair, was a man who now stood up.

'Thank you, Rosanna,' he said. He was tall and thin, with an odd sort of face that matched his body. They both looked like they had been stretched, pulled from top and bottom so that they had elongated. He had a long nose and long chin and eyes that seemed too close together.

'I'm Collodi,' he said, holding out his pencil-like fingers. 'I'm Mr Di Angelo's personal lawyer.'

'Castagnetti,' I said.

'Please,' he said, motioning towards another armchair.

I sat down and looked around the room. It was the sort of study that was used more for discreet meetings than for scholarship. Books were there not for research or reading but for sound proofing.

'Mr Di Angelo will be with us shortly.' He looked at his watch. 'He's always behind schedule,' he said apologetically.

We made idle conversation as we waited for Di Angelo. It was another ten minutes before he came in: a short man with a round, boyish face. His suit disguised a well-fed stomach, and his fingers were like sausages. He bounded towards me as if he wanted to embrace.

'Castagnetti, right? You're a private investigator, is that what I hear? Very exciting.'

We shook hands and he took my hand in two of his, looking up at me. He had curly, greying hair and teeth that must have been professionally whitened.

'Very exciting job, yours.' He was unstoppable. 'Must take you all over the country, chasing leads and criminals. All that gadgetry and surveillance and software. I've hired one or two in my time and they certainly run up the clock, eh? What do you charge?'

'Three hundred a day.'

'You're cheap. Are you any good?'

I nodded. 'I get the job done. What's your day rate?'

He smiled bashfully, raising his palms to gesture he didn't know. 'Depends.'

'And are you any good?' I asked.

He smiled, a gleeful smile that looked like he was ready to attack. 'Yeah, I can see you're good at your job. Antonio, get him a drink. What will you have Castagnetti?'

'Mint julep.'

'Mint julep, eh?' He gave me a thump on the arm. 'Hear that,

Antonio? The guy drinks exotic, American stuff. You know how to mix that up?'

The lawyer nodded and went over to a drinks cabinet by the window. Di Angelo had his head to one side and was still smiling at me.

'Sit down, sit down.'

I went back to the same chair.

'What's this about, Castagnetti?' He kept saying my name like he was trying to be my best friend.

'I've been hired by a couple to find their daughter. She went missing a day or two ago.'

He was still smiling, but listening intently.

'It seems she's with a man called Fabrizio Mori. A small-time hustler who's done time for extortion in the past. He's got a grey ponytail. Sometimes uses his brother's passport.'

'And what's any of this got to do with me?'

'I think he's already made contact with your people, which is why Tony Vespa was rifling through his caravan the other day. I think your people are trying to find him before he finds you.'

His lips had closed around his big teeth now. He was still grinning but was watching me like he didn't want to be my friend any more.

'Do you know anything about this, Antonio?' he asked.

The lawyer turned round, holding a tumbler. He shook his head.

'Why would a hustler abduct a girl and contact me?' Di Angelo was watching me with shrewd eyes. All his bonhomie was gone now.

'The girl, Simona Biondi, is the daughter of a liaison set up to boost your viewing figures. Her mother, Chiara, was one of

Vespa's call girls, one of those young bodies used to pleasure advertisers and the like. Only Chiara was sent to Giorgio Gregori, the then head of Teleshare and the man responsible for calculating viewing figures across the peninsula. He got what he wanted, and in return you got to choose who should be in his sample of representative viewers. The more viewers, the more money you could charge advertisers.'

The lawyer came over and placed a drink in my hand as though he wasn't listening. It smelt nicely of mint and I took a deep sip as I watched Di Angelo. He was standing there, in the middle of the room, frowning at the rug.

'The girl,' I said, 'is living evidence of the collusion between your business empire and Teleshare. Evidence that for years the viewing figures have been inflated so that you could overcharge advertisers. My guess is that Mori is hoping you'll pay his rent for a few years in return for his silence.'

Di Angelo looked like a man who was wondering why he was always the victim. He was chuckling silently to himself as if amused by the folly of other people, at their ability to misunderstand him. I decided to play to his sense of victimisation.

'This man Mori is blackmailing you. If you haven't heard of it, it's because your people are keeping it from you, trying to protect you from bad news. This man is trying to wound you and your business.'

He looked at me suddenly, like all he cared about was the fact that we might be able to save our nascent friendship. 'You've got quite an imagination, Castagnetti.'

'And you've got quite a reputation.'

'For what?'

'For fantasy. For creativity. All those things that make our country great.' The man was so vain he didn't seem to realise I was buttering him both sides. 'You're not one of the dullards who trudge along in life. You seize any opportunity, shake it, throw it around until it submits to your will and opens up vast avenues of new opportunity. Nothing can stand in your way. You make up the rules as you go along.'

'My client,' the lawyer said from his chair, 'always obeys the law.'

'Of course. But when one's in politics,' I raised my glass in the senator's direction, 'one has to obey more than the law. In politics you have to obey the whims of public morality too. And the puritans and hypocrites in the press and the judiciary,' I tried to stay on his side, 'will use anything to slay a man's reputation. That's why Mori's seen his moment. He knows you're vulnerable now.'

'I always said you should never have gone into politics,' the lawyer said. 'It doubles the number of enemies.'

'Enemies?' Di Angelo looked astonished. 'I don't have any enemies. Why would anyone be my enemy?'

'Because you're in politics,' the lawyer said quickly. 'Because you're powerful.'

'But that means I can help people. That's why they love me.'

'Of course.' The lawyer was being sarcastic now. 'Tell us why you really went into politics.'

Di Angelo smiled. 'They have the most beautiful mistresses.'

'That's why you went into politics?' I asked.

'Sure. Listen, Castagnetti, when you've got a TV channel there are always hundreds of people asking you to put their daughter or mistress on screen. It seems like every girl in the peninsula wants to slip into a sequinned bikini and prance around under the lights. And to satisfy these girls, their fathers or lovers all come to me and try and persuade me that their little darling would be perfect for this or that show. You ignore most of them, but there are some you can't ignore. Because they've got the most beautiful mistresses, and they've got the power to pull the plug on your operation.'

'The politicians?'

'Right. I realised that was where the real power was. I realised that if I had the studios and a slice of the Senate, no one would tell me who to hire, or what to broadcast. And,' he smiled, 'I thought I might even get myself a beautiful mistress.'

'Did you?'

'More than I could ever dream of. Ambitious women are drawn to powerful men like kids to ice cream. They want a taste of what we've got.'

'A taste, eh?'

'And in a way, there's not that much difference between a parliament and a TV studio. In both you're trying to give the public images and ideas. You're trying to show them how incredible the world could be. And, in both, we're bound to give people what they want. We research meticulously what our audience desires and we try to fulfil those desires. We're realising their dreams.'

'Is that the real audience or the fake one?'

He smiled slightly. 'We're realising their dreams,' he repeated.

'You're realising your dreams. You're getting rich while they sit there passively on the sofa, their eyeballs sprayed with ads.'

'That's a very cynical view of our creative industry.'

'Creative.' I repeated the word. 'Creative cuts many ways.'

He looked at me and flashed a smile. 'What is it you want exactly, Castagnetti?'

'I'm not interested in your creativity, past or present. No interest in what went on in your empire in years gone by. All I want, Senator,' I tried to put as much respect and solemnity in my voice as possible, 'is to take a young girl home to her parents.'

'Of course. Of course. I'm a parent myself, I can understand their anxiety. How can we help you?'

'I need to know the next time Mori gets in touch. I need to pick up his trail.'

'This Mori,' he said, turning to his lawyer, 'have you heard of him?'

The man shook his head, acting dumb.

'Vespa had,' I said quickly. 'He was round at Mori's place when I was there. He gave me a facial,' I pointed to the bruising on my face. 'If Mori gets in touch again, I want to know.'

'You got a card?'

I passed over one of my dog-eared cards. He looked at it and then slapped it against the palm of his hand as if to check its authenticity. He passed it over to the lawyer.

'We'll do everything we can to help you, Castagnetti,' he said, offering his hand. As we shook, he moved his arm hard towards the door, pushing my hand away from him as if to signal that my time was up.

'Just one thing,' I said. 'This case I'm working on . . . it's just a hunch, but something tells me it's linked to another case from years ago. There was a young girl who went missing in the early nineties called Anna Sartori. Remember her?'

He looked over his shoulder as if interrogating his memory. He shook his head.

'Anna Sartori,' I said again.

He shifted his gaze slightly. 'Rings a vague bell.'

'She had been hustling with this Mori character. And then moved up in the world, servicing some of your business partners. She was about to get a go as a showgirl. What happened?'

Di Angelo frowned and rubbed his forehead with his thumb and fingers. 'We have thousands of aspiring showgirls every year. I can't remember all the ups and downs of each one's career.'

'I heard she was the squeeze of one of your main advertisers. Some yogurt magnate.'

'Baroni?' He smiled to himself. 'Yeah, that's right. Baroni. I remember now. He had got the hots for that bird. Really lost his head over her. Kept phoning me up to ask for her to get her break. You know, when a man who is pumping millions into your company makes a request, you have to listen. The guy was one of our largest advertisers.'

'So you agreed to promote her onto one of your shows.'

'Yeah. She was cute, had a nice smile, decent curves. I wanted to keep Baroni onside, so she was taken on.'

'How do you mean?'

'We agreed to put her on one of the shows. You know, a bit of a female frame to the picture, something to keep us weak men amused.' He smiled as if the lewd linked us all.

'But she never went on screen. She was dumped.'

'Yeah. That man, Mori, showed up with a box of snaps. Photos of the girl doing her stuff with half the A-listers of Rome. Even I learnt some stuff looking at those snaps.' He laughed, shaking his head. 'We couldn't have one of our show-girls, the public face of our channel, with that sort of profile.'

'I thought they all had that sort of past.'

'Sure they do,' he said. 'Sure they do. It's just not all captured on film.' Di Angelo chuckled to himself.

'So Anna had a past and you didn't like it. But she knew you had a past too.'

'We all have a past,' he said.

I watched him, wondering whether it was worth letting on what I thought must have happened to her. I couldn't ima-gine someone like Anna giving up without a fight. She would have tried every trick in the book, and she knew them all. She knew her friend Chiara Biondi was being used by Tony Vespa and Mario Di Angelo to keep the head of Teleshare onside. In return for a few carnal pleasures, Giorgio Gregori was deliber-ately bumping up viewing figures and allowing Di Angelo to double and treble his ad rates. Sartori knew what was going on and must have used it as ammunition when the studio was threatening to offload her.

'Not many people have got a past quite like yours. When you dumped her, Sartori threatened to make your cosy relationship with Teleshare public, make it known that your fantastic view-ing figures were a fantasy, simply payback for the girls you used to serve up for Gregori.'

He looked at me with disappointment. There was none of the expected anger or defensiveness, only disappointment and, if anything, wry amusement.

'You think, Detective, that I had something to do with her disappearance?'

'Did you?'

'Antonio,' he said to his lawyer with a lethal grin, 'you put too much hard stuff in the detective's drink. It's gone to his head.'

'What happened to Anna Sartori?' I asked.

He spun round quickly, staring at me. His face was stern now, almost unrecognisable from the fun-loving, boyish rogue he had been a few minutes before. Now his eyelids were low, like he was tired of the world and of me. 'I'm used to gossip and allegations,' he said. 'Happens all the time in this country where the imagination runs wild. Especially because people like to think that they would be just as successful as me if only they weren't honest. They put my success down to dishonesty because it makes their failure easier to live with. It happens all the time. It reassures them that their jinxed lives are down to their saintly morality, rather than their dull, boring, predictable, bourgeois provincialism. You remember what Andreotti said once? "Apart from the Punic wars, I've been accused of everything." Well, it's the same with me, Detective. I've been accused of just about everything. Every week there's a new investigation into some part of my business. Isn't that right, Antonio?' He bounced his head at the lawyer. 'He works an eighteen-hour day every day just to defend me from accusation and insinuation. And he costs a lot more than your three hundred a day. So nothing surprises me any more. I'm used to it. I'm used to incompetent investigators seeing me as a scalp. You want to know what happened to Anna Sartori? She probably committed suicide because she couldn't make it as a star. End of story.'

'End of scandal, you mean?'

He put his chin on his shoulder like he was praying for patience. 'If you find out what happened to her, let me know.

Because then I can make it public and people like you might stop trying to pin every crime on my person.' He looked at me briefly. 'Now get out.'

The lawyer stood up, ready to usher me through the door in case I didn't make my own way.

'Let me know when Mori gets in touch,' I said. I didn't hold out much hope.

I walked the couple of blocks back to the car. I was feeling melancholic. I leant over the balustrades of the river and watched the grey-brown water flowing slowly to the sea. There were a few boats down there, the water lapping at their hulls and making a gentle slapping noise. A few gulls swept down on invisible fish.

The drive to Baroni's house was slow. The roads were full of flash, static cars. The noise of horns and radios and shouted insults was part of the soundtrack of the capital, and I sat there with the window down, getting so used to the noise it was almost hypnotic. I pulled up outside Baroni's address. I was surprised to see a dull block of flats. I had assumed an industrialist would have had a large villa, but this block looked, as they say, popular: there were football flags and laundry flapping from balconies, rusty bikes hanging on the railings, their wheels badly bent from hooligans having used them as a trampoline.

'Who is it?' said a gravelly voice at the citofono.

'Castagnetti.'

'Who?' The voice sounded impatient, even aggressive.

'I'm a private detective. Is that Mr Baroni?'

'It is.'

'Could I ask you a couple of questions?'

'About what?'

'Anna Sartori.'

The line went quiet.

'Dottore?' I said deferentially, not sure he was still there.

'I'll come down.'

A few minutes later I heard the gate click. I looked up and saw an elderly man who was pressing the gate-release button from inside the palazzo. He was a smallish, thin man wearing a tie and a V-neck red sweater. He looked fit but tired. His hair was jet black, probably dyed, I thought. He must have been in his sixties. He walked towards me slowly, looking left and right as if checking who else was around before opening the outer gate and looking at me with real intent.

'Let's walk,' was all he said.

We crossed the road and went into a small park. It was dusk, but the park was still noisy with the shrieks of young children. We stood side by side watching a young woman pushing a child on a swing.

'A private detective, eh?'

'That's right.'

'Who hired you?' His voice was strong and stern, the sort of voice that was used to cutting to the chase.

'It's just personal interest.'

'That so?'

'That's right.'

We watched a young toddler being helped up the steps of a slide by her grandfather.

'Why now?'

'New facts are emerging.'

'Like what?'

I shrugged, not wanting to give him everything up front. I needed chips to bargain with.

'Like what?' he repeated, louder this time.

'Like what was happening to her in the weeks before she went missing.' We hadn't even said her name. I had only mentioned it once on the intercom.

'Go on.'

'I heard you knew her quite well.'

He turned to look at me, moving his whole torso as if his neck were too stiff to rotate just his head. His lips were pursed, like he was about to defend himself.

'Sure. I knew her, knew her well enough.'

He was still talking in code. I let him know I had broken it.

'I heard you were lovers.'

'You heard? What do you know about what we were?'

'The way I heard it, it was quite a love story.'

He said nothing but stared straight ahead, watching the children chasing each other underneath the steps of the slide.

'Sit down,' he said, motioning towards a bench facing the park. We sat side by side, staring ahead.

'How do you know? Who told you?'

'One of Anna's friends. And Di Angelo confirmed it.'

'Di Angelo? You've spoken to him?'

'Briefly.'

Baroni looked at me now, like he could take me more seriously if Di Angelo had seen me.

'You married?' he asked.

'No.'

'Marriage is an odd thing. You promise to spend the rest of your life with someone at an age when you don't even know what love is. And chances are you spend the rest of your life falling in love with other people and trying not to hurt your wife. That's all love is in the end – the hope that you will avoid hurting someone.'

'Did your wife know about Anna?'

Out of the corner of my eye I saw him shrug. 'My wife never knew. Or maybe she did, but she never let me know she knew. When you've been married forty-odd years there are plenty of secrets and this was one of ours. I'm sure she's got hers.'

'What happened to fidelity?'

'Fidelity?' He chuckled, as though such a naïve question didn't deserve a reply. Then he paused and thought, and gave me one. 'Fidelity is like an ice cube. It'll survive in the freezer, but will disappear in the sun.'

'So Anna was your sun? Or one of them?'

'Nobody wants to live their life in a freezer.'

'What was she like?'

He sighed heavily. 'She was beautiful. Very beautiful.' I turned to look at him and his stare shifted to the distance. 'You've seen the photos of her?' He looked mildly pained, as if an old wound was making him wince. 'And her beauty wasn't just her youth.

'There was an innocence about her. Don't get me wrong, I knew she was a pro. She knew men, there's no doubt she knew exactly what she was doing physically, if you see what I mean. She was an expert there. But she was like a young girl too. Always wanting ice cream, or to go to the seaside, or insisting we stop to look at dolls in a children's shop.'

This time he shook his head, smiling. 'She was a beautiful, simple girl. She was barely more than a child, really. She had that childish spontaneity, wanting to do silly things on the spur of the moment. She would go all soppy when she saw an animal in the street. Would always want to stop and pat the puppy and talk to the owners about what it was called and so on. She was like that, like a little girl. I heard she had never known her father and, well, I think she liked me because I was gentle with her, I treated her like a daughter. She used to want me to read to her in bed, read her stories and so on.' He shook his head again, laughing quietly like he had wanted to do other things in bed. 'But really she was quite a sad little girl. She constantly felt that the real action was elsewhere, that she was missing out on something, she was in the wrong place. So she was restless, suddenly leaving on a whim or rolling up on another. She couldn't concentrate on anything for more than a few minutes, before getting bored.'

'I heard she was pretty single-minded.'

He looked at me and then shifted focus, so that he seemed to be looking through me and into the distant past. 'The only thing she was focused on was getting on screen. It was an obsession for her. It's all she could talk about sometimes. When she was feeling optimistic, she would describe what her life would be like when she was a diva, the demands she would make on her staff. She used to joke that I would be her chauffeur when she was a star. It was a part she practised for years, a part that made her feel fulfilled: one day, she thought, she would be recognised in the street, would offer her fingers for people to kiss. She used to act it all out for me. I found it embarrassing, rather silly to be honest. But it was her driving ambition, to become this acknowledged beauty, this recognisable icon. She would prance around the bedroom pretending to be carrying large bags from expensive shops – no, she said I would be carrying her bags – and would be phoning her famous friends, calling the other stars by their first names and inviting them to lunch.'

'Was it ever likely to happen?'

He shrugged. 'I did my best. I spoke to the people at the station. I was a big investor into their operation and they listened to me. And Anna would do anything asked of her. She wanted to go places, and she could be quite a cat when she needed to be. She had claws all right. I met her at one of the parties the TV station used to throw for advertisers and she didn't seem all that innocent there, I can say that much.'

'What do you mean?'

'She was using her charms.'

'Meaning?'

'She was flirting, giggling, imploring. She wanted to get on TV. That's what all those girls cared about. That's why they did what they did.'

'Which was?'

'What do you think? They were there to oil the wheels of business. We all knew that. Di Angelo used to lay them on by the coach load. And they, poor things, thought they were just a step away from the big time.'

'I thought she was about to get her break, to get into one of the chorus lines.'

'Yeah,' he chortled derisively. 'She pushed real hard for that. Went on and on at me. Made me go and talk to Di Angelo every week. She wanted me to threaten to pull our advertising from his channel unless she got her break.'

'Did you?'

'What?'

'Threaten to pull your advertising?'

'I liked her. I did what I could for her and that meant she liked me. Di Angelo even promised to put her forward, but then his promises were like raw spaghetti. Easily broken.'

'But she thought she was about to be taken on?'

'That was the way Di Angelo always played it. "Your big break is just round the corner" and all that. She thought she had been chosen to replace some girl.' He shrugged. 'Came to see me all ecstatic, hugging me, kissing me, thanking me for getting her her big break. She was about to be offered a contract. Everything she had ever wanted was about to come true. After all the demeaning parties, all the broken promises. It never happened.'

'Because Mori turned up with prints of her past?'

'Right,' he looked at me, surprised how much I knew. 'This guy from her past had turned up with all sorts of snaps. Intimate stuff. That's what she told me. Came to me distraught saying that the studio manager had told her it wouldn't have suited the image of the channel. You know, behind the scenes it was all sordid orgies, but the public image was one of healthy families watching innocent game shows.'

'So she never got her break?'

He shook his head. 'And it broke her. She had done so much to get that far, and then at the last minute it had all been snatched away from her. She was white with anger when she came into my office. That's when I really saw those claws. Said she would get revenge on everyone, would bring down the whole empire.'

'How was she going to do that?'

'She was smart. Childish but smart. She wanted to go public

with the links between Di Angelo's studio and Teleshare. Told me she had proof that the viewing figures were being fiddled. She was feeling vengeful. But she was trying to take revenge on people who were stronger than her. So she got hurt.'

'Di Angelo?'

Baroni threw his hands out in front of him, as if to say that he didn't know. A child's ball had rolled under our bench and a little boy ran towards us, pausing at the sight of us. I reached under and got the green sponge ball and threw it towards him. He put his hands eagerly together, trying to catch it, but it bounced off his chest and back towards me. I threw it again and this time he caught it.

'She said,' the old man began slowly, 'that if they had dirt on her, she had plenty on them.'

'On the studio?'

'Right.'

He was still staring at the young boy with the ball. 'The channel used to sort out girls for the head of Teleshare.'

'So I heard.'

'Anna knew all about it and she wasn't daft. She knew that it meant Teleshare was inflating viewing figures. And she knew why they were doing it. If you've got an extra million viewers you can charge much more for advertising. The viewing figures dictate the cost of ad space. Laying on girls for that monster was an easy way to increase revenue.'

'Didn't that increase your costs? You were one of the major advertisers on the channel.'

'That's why Anna came to me. She was smart. She thought I would be appalled about overpaying and would fight her corner.'

There was something in the way he said it that sounded strange. It sounded like he wasn't appalled, like he wasn't going to fight her corner. I could understand him possibly not sticking up for a young girl, but I was sure any hard-nosed businessman would stick up for his business. If he was being overcharged for advertising to reach phantom viewers he would have fought back. It sounded as though he didn't fight at all.

'Why weren't you?'

'What?'

'Appalled.'

He must have realised he had let slip something. He didn't reply but just sat there staring into space.

'You weren't incensed that the channel had invented tens or hundreds of thousands of viewers to inflate your costs?'

He turned round to look at me, defiance etched in the deep lines of his face. 'I probably was appalled. I don't remember.'

He sat there with both palms on his knees now, leaning forward. He looked more animated, more anxious, than he had been so far.

'Why weren't you appalled at being overcharged for advertising?'

'Let it go,' he said.

If he had been younger I would have put my knuckles through his teeth. Instead I decided to put them through his marriage.

'Your wife at home?'

'What are you talking about?'

'I believe in honesty. Give me the truth or I'll give it to her.'

He turned round very slowly. 'Leave her out of this.'

I stood up. 'I'm going to have a chat with your wife.'

'Sit down,' he barked. He took a deep breath and I listened to him exhaling angrily. He was still leaning forward, but his chin was on his left shoulder so that he was addressing my feet.

'I knew exactly what was going on. All of us knew. Di Angelo didn't have one point three million viewers, or whatever they said it was back then. It was impossible. For the crap he broadcast he was lucky to get half that. And we all knew Teleshare was in his pocket.' The words were coming fast, like he wanted to get the confession out quickly. 'I was overpaying because I was getting a rebate. That was what he called it. "A rebate".'

He looked up at me sheepishly to check I had understood. I got it all right. It was an old ploy: inflate invoices to a company that can then reduce its profits and tax liabilities. And the person in the company who pays the inflated invoices then gets a cash rebate back. It normally goes in their pocket rather than the company coffers. It suits everyone except the company's shareholders but they never know about it anyway. It was as if everything was being inflated: viewing figures, invoices, reputations. It would have only taken a pointed object to deflate the lot and Anna Sartori had been sharpening her claws.

'So what did you tell Anna?'

'I told her I would help her.' He was breathing deeply now, holding his forehead in his right hand.

'And what did you actually do?'

'I phoned Di Angelo. I told him that Anna knew about everything and that she was flapping at the mouth. I told him that he needed to deal with the situation.'

'What does that mean? "Deal with the situation"?'

'I expected him to come to an agreement with her. Offer her

money, give her back her place on the chorus line. I don't know. That was his job. I expected him to come to a solution.'

'What was his suggestion?'

'He told me to send Anna round to the Hotel del Fiume. He assured me he would sort everything out.'

'So you arranged for Anna to see Di Angelo?'

'I don't know if she saw him, or who she saw. That was just where she was headed.'

I sat with my shoulders against the back of the bench, staring at the skyline. Baroni had effectively sent his lover to an appointment, after which she had never been seen again. He had warned Di Angelo about her desire for revenge and, it seemed, Di Angelo – or one of his cronies – had struck first.

'I had no idea that was going to happen to her,' he said slowly. 'We were very close. I was very fond of her. Very fond.'

'But you fed her to the lions.'

'I thought they might give her back her place in the studio. That they would give her some money. I thought something good would come out of it. I never, never for one minute . . . There's not one day I haven't mourned her.' He was talking fast now. 'Not one day that I haven't had to carry around this terrible weight of what happened.'

'What did happen?'

'I don't know. I don't know. I only know she went missing. Wasn't seen again. And from that day I never again gave any money to Di Angelo's mob. I cancelled all advertising contracts with his studio.'

'You never confronted him about Anna?'

'I tried. I asked him, the same as the police and the journalists and everyone else. He just smiled and shrugged and insisted it was nothing to do with him.'

'And you believed him?'

'I didn't know what to believe any more.'

We sat like that for a few minutes. My guess, at least, had been right. Sartori wouldn't be ousted without a fight, and she knew enough secrets to put the wind up the studio's bosses. I hadn't known about the inflated invoices, but that was almost standard practice in the TV industry.

'Do you remember where Anna was from?' I asked.

'Sure. She used to talk about it all the time. Pretended she hated the place, but was proud of it at the same time. A bit like her self-esteem: one minute you thought she despised herself, and at other times she was proud of herself, strong, you know.'

'What was it called?'

'What?'

'The village she was from?'

'Visso.'

I stood up and shook his hand. He looked at me briefly before going back to staring into the distance.

Back in the hotel, I took out my old atlas of the peninsula. It was to the north-east of the capital, in a remote part of Le Marche. I looked at the map and saw that the roads around Visso were mostly thin, meandering lines between large green patches and steep slopes. It looked like it was way up in forested mountains.

I got up early the next day, but the drive was still slow and hot. It took me over an hour to escape the city and another to find the right road heading out east. I stopped in an Autogrill and got a piadina and a coffee. The people at the bar were arguing about the football transfer market and whether Lazio needed a new left-sided player.

I felt tired. I had been at it non-stop and just needed to sleep for a few days. Through the haze I could see the blurry outline of the mountains getting slowly closer. The road criss-crossed a river, following it along one bank and then the other. As it became narrower the road entered tunnels open on one side, so that you could see the river through the vertical concrete pillars. There was hardly any other traffic and it was a relief to be in the wilderness after the crowded chaos of the capital.

Eventually, I got close to the village. The road bent back on itself again and again as it zigzagged up towards an ever-receding summit. There were stacks of drying wood by the roadside and lonely houses in the distance.

The village wasn't much more than a couple of hundred houses huddling close to the small square. There was one shop and a bar and that was it. It felt like the kind of place a stranger would stick out.

'Salve!' I shouted at the barman as I walked in. 'Grappa, please.'

'Subito.'

I looked around at a couple of ruddy faces that were staring at me from a table in the corner.

'Morning,' I said in their direction. They nodded almost imperceptibly, like they blamed me for disturbing their slumber.

'Prego.' The barman put a thin glass on the chrome bar. I raised it off the bar and held it towards him, in a silent salute, and sank it. The liquid burnt pleasantly as the poison sank into my stomach.

'I'm looking for someone,' I said quietly. 'The mother of Anna Sartori.'

'Anna Sartori?' He frowned, his grey eyebrows coming low over his eyes.

'She went missing in Rome back in the early nineties.'

He started nodding slowly as though it were coming back to him. 'Anna Sartori. I know. It was a big story twenty years ago. Used to have all sorts poking around here.'

'Does her mother still live in the village?'

'She used to live down in that house on the main road. Haven't seen her for years.'

'Which house?'

He described where it was, just next to the main road back down the hillside. I slapped a few coins on the counter and got back in the car. I could see the house from up here, just as he had described it: a grey place by the slip road that led to the hairpins. I zigzagged back down, wondering what I would find.

The place looked unkempt and eccentric from the outside.

There were three or four cats crawling between broken terra-cotta pots. A vegetable patch was untended, only the conical bamboo poles for beans were still standing, tied together at the top by a piece of fraying twine. There were the dried remnants of last year's tomato plants. I walked around the back, but there wasn't much there, only a few metres of concrete before a fence dividing the property from a large field of wheat.

'Anyone around?' I shouted.

The front door had frosted glass and flattened steel slats. I couldn't see a doorbell. I tried to knock on the glass but my fist wouldn't fit between the grey slats. The door was open so I walked in, asking again if anyone was around. I heard the sound of a television, of a presenter's voice floating above the eager applause of his audience. I followed the sound and saw, at the end of a corridor, a woman sitting on a sofa.

'Permesso,' I shouted loudly.

She turned and saw me, leant on the arm of the sofa and pushed herself up. She was a short, round woman, the sort who didn't care for her appearance. Her hair was unbrushed and grey, and she was wearing an apron over her floral dress. The pattern looked the same as the throws on the sofa.

'What are you after?' she said with the blunt suspicion of the countryside.

'Are you the mother of Anna Sartori?' I asked.

She looked at me with stern eyes like I was trespassing on private grief. She nodded.

I introduced myself, told her my name and my profession. She just stared at me, her suspicion growing as I spoke. 'Do you mind if I ask you some questions?'

'Why?'

'A young girl has gone missing in Rome. Her parents have hired me to look for her. It seems she's involved with the same crowd as your daughter was a few years back.'

'What crowd was that?' She stared at me without moving. A cat came in and nuzzled her ankle, its tail curling round her thick calf. Her hands were on her hips like she was reluctant to give me any access to her life.

'Fabrizio Mori.'

Her face tensed up as she looked at the mouldy wall beside her. 'Mori,' she repeated.

'The girl he's got is only eighteen. She might be in danger and anything you can tell me about him, and about your daughter, might help me find her.'

She stared at me, trying to weigh up if it was worth it. Eventually, she offered me a coffee, a sign she was content for me to be there.

There were two cats on the kitchen table, both licking at an unfinished meal. She ignored them and went over to the sink where there was a stack of plates that looked like something from a cartoon: a column of white ceramics bending left and right as it rose far above the level of the taps. She found the macchinetta for a coffee, unscrewed it and started rinsing it out. The whole place felt as if she had let it go, like she couldn't be bothered to tidy or clean any more. When the coffee was ready and she opened the fridge to get some milk, there was almost nothing in there. It was refrigerating only air, the illuminated white insides a reminder of her poverty.

'Have you got children?' she asked, passing me a small, chipped cup of coffee.

I shook my head.

was strange: even in that image of an innocent child, omething melancholic, something that suggested n underdog and would have to fight for her

'Anna was my only child.'

I nodded slowly to show that I understood grief. I had lost my parents before I was in double figures, so I knew all about it.

'Nothing you can do,' she said, 'will be of any help to Anna or me.'

'It might stop it happening to someone else.'

'It? What's "it"?'

I could tell this was going to be difficult. She was spiky and suspicious, not keen for an outsider to barge into her house and start asking questions.

'The disappearance.'

'Her disappearance?' she said quickly. 'Anna's dead.'

'You're probably right.'

'Only it's even worse than that because they've never let me have the body. You can't mourn properly if you don't even know, with that terrible certainty, that she really is dead. You know it, but you dread it, and avoid it. Even now, I sometimes find myself still hoping she might just be in South America or Paris, happily living her life surrounded by lots of children.'

'Who's "they"?'

'What?'

'You said they've never let you have the body. Who do you blame?'

She looked at me defensively as if she realised she had already said too much. She pretended to be distracted, looking at her hands and wiping them on her apron. She bent down to pick up the cat that was still mewing at her ankles, turning it over like a baby to stroke its soft, downy stomach. I looked at her face: she had the wrinkles of a lifelong smoker and grieving mother. But there were still hints of the beauty she had passed on to Anna: dark eyes, high, round cheeks. When she looked up at me, she realised I was waiting for an answer.

'"They"?' I said. 'Who's "they"?'

'I don't know. I know nothing more about it than you do. I read afterwards that she was involved with that TV studio, that she had got involved with little parties where she had met powerful people. That maybe she knew too much.'

'Did the authorities speak to you?'

She shrugged like she was unimpressed. 'They came here once. Asked a couple of questions and left. Everything I've found out about the investigation I've had to beg for. They never shared any information with me and I can't afford to retain a lawyer to badger them. After those first few months, the only scraps of information I got were from journalists.'

'What did you hear?'

'I told you,' she sounded impatient. 'Anna was involved in parties and the like. That she must have discovered something.'

I looked round the room. There was cat hair on all the cushions and an ashtray overflowing with stubs. There seemed to be a film of dust everywhere except on a photograph of a young, dark-haired girl missing her two front teeth.

'Is that Anna?'

'It is.' She went over and picked up the frame and passed it over.

It was strange: even in that image of an innocent child, there was something melancholic, something that suggested she knew she was an underdog and would have to fight for her future.

'Let me show you her room,' the woman said. I watched her

walking slowly, shuffling her slippers along the floor as if she lacked the energy to pick up her feet. I wondered how she made ends meet.

She led me into a small bedroom with the blinds down. She flicked on the light and I saw a room frozen in time. It looked like something from the late eighties: posters of Patrick Swayze and Bruce Willis, photos of friends with big hair and big shoulder pads. There was a satchel, brightly coloured notebooks with schoolgirl doodles, a few cassettes.

'I've still got all her clothes,' the woman said, walking past me with the cat and opening a wardrobe.

I looked at the dresses, the stonewashed shorts and the denim jacket.

'I just can't get rid of them,' the woman said, her voice beginning to give way. 'It would be like giving up on her.' She sighed heavily. 'I tried not to clean it for years, just to keep her smell, but even that has gone now. The cats come in and sleep on her bed and . . . there's nothing left of her here. No trace at all.'

'I'm sorry,' I said slowly. I looked around, not wanting to rush the questioning. It seemed like something from a museum – a snapshot of what used to be fashionable a couple of decades ago.

'How did she meet Mori?'

The woman's eyes glazed over like she was looking far into the past. 'He's from a village the other side of the river. There's not much social life round here and the youngsters all meet up in local bars and clubs. They had friends in common. He said he thought she could become a model,' she shook her head in dismay.

'I heard she was very beautiful.'

'She was.' She nodded. 'Very beautiful. But she was naïve. She didn't realise that a man with a camera might have other motives.'

'What motives did he have?'

She gave me a weary look. 'The usual. He wanted to charm her, seduce her.'

'Was he much older?'

'A few years. She was sixteen when they met and he was in his early twenties. Not much difference, but that's light years at that age. She was an innocent and he was like a snake in the grass. The first time I saw him I knew he was trouble. He picked her up from here and didn't even come in and introduce himself. So I went out, wanting to have a look at him, and it was obvious to me he was up to no good. He was charming, all signora this and signora that, but I saw through him.'

'And what did you see?'

'A man who thought my daughter was his ticket to the big time.' She looked wistfully round the room and then motioned with her head that we should leave it in peace. I followed her back to the living room with its one floral sofa.

We sat next to each other on the sofa, sitting so close that it was easier to talk to each other staring ahead at the TV and the table.

'They were together for a while,' the woman went on, reminiscing about her daughter's lost innocence. 'We argued about it. I thought he was inappropriate and told her so. He was her first love, the first man in her life, and she thought he could do no wrong. So we argued and, one day, she just left.'

'Why did you say the first man in her life? What happened to her father?'

The woman let out a derisive sigh. 'He legged it long before she was born.' I could see her out of the corner of my eye, shaking her head. 'That's why I was so hard on her when Mori came sniffing around. I didn't want history to repeat itself.'

'What history?'

'What happened to me,' she said, raising her voice slightly.

I waited, not wanting to push her back to a painful past. 'Which was?'

I could hear her breathing. Another cat came in and leapt on the table. 'I was charmed by a man. Some student who was here on holiday with friends. I barely knew what was happening until it was too late.' We watched the cat in silence for a while, seeing it arch its back and raise its tail as if a puppeteer had tensioned all its strings.

'That was back in the seventies,' she said. 'A single, pregnant girl in the countryside back then was a pariah. People thought I was stupid, loose, immoral. I was treated like I was a murderer. People actually spat at me when I pushed Anna round the village. It was like my life was over. My parents had died, I had no job and no prospect of marriage, and the only thing I had in the world was my little girl. My beautiful, precious, bubbly little girl.'

I looked at her and nodded.

'That's all she was when Mori arrived in his flash car, a little girl. And I could see everything starting over again. So I did everything I could to stop it, and that only pushed her further away until,' her voice broke, suddenly going high-pitched. She stopped abruptly as if silence was the only way to dam the tears.

I looked down at her hand and put mine over it, wrapping my fingers round her loose skin. Her other hand immediately gripped my forearm like I was the only thing keeping her afloat. We sat like that for a while, strangers clinging on to each other.

It sounded as if she had unwittingly lost the prospects and possibilities of her own youth. She had been scorned and shunned, and then the only thing she had in the world, her precious child, had been taken away. And had then gone missing. I stared at the muted TV, watching the fake cheerfulness. It seemed like a distorted mirror of the woman's sorrow.

'Why do you care?' she said after a while.

I repeated to her that I was looking for a young girl. That that was my job.

'Seems more than a job,' she said, staring at me.

I looked back at the TV, not wanting to admit it was true. But I knew I was in this game because I had seen too many children lose their families and vice versa. And since I'd never had a family, I was on a mission to put others back together. I met hundreds of kids who had lost their parents, if they had ever had them. Or parents who had lost their kids because of the usual addictions and weaknesses. This job was my way of putting the pieces back together, of trying to reunite families before it was too late. Maybe that's why this woman and I seemed to have a bond.

'Where did they go?' I asked her.

'Rome.' She was shaking her head. 'Mori had put an idea in her head that she could be a showgirl. It became an obsession for her. She wanted to be on TV, to become a star. It got to the stage where she was prepared to sacrifice anything for that ambition.'

'Including herself?'

She looked at me sharply. 'She would never have committed suicide. Someone wanted her out of the way.'

I must have looked doubtful, because she started telling me about how her daughter had been scared in the days before her death. 'She knew too much about certain men in positions of power. She was at all their little parties and when she didn't get what she wanted, she threatened to expose their sordid world. And the next thing I knew, she was missing. I would rather,' she had a sharp intake of breath, 'know she were dead than have this. This uncertainty, this terror that any day the worst is still to come. I still can't mourn her properly.'

I said nothing to contradict her. It was possible Anna had paid the price for threatening to spill some dirty beans. But it seemed just as likely that she had taken too much bad gear and gone the way of so many aspiring starlets before her. Someone may have just chucked her in the Tiber after an overdose.

'Did Anna ever mention to you the people she was seeing in Rome? The jobs she was doing?'

She shook her head, staring at her feet. 'We were barely speaking to each other back then. She knew what I thought of what she was doing with her life. And I knew what she thought of what I had done with mine.' She looked up at me. 'We had grown so far apart . . .' She trailed off, her eyes losing focus as she stared at the wall opposite.

'No names, no mention of anyone in particular?'

She shook her head slowly, her stare still lost in the distance. 'I don't see that I can really help you. It was so long ago.'

'Mori's still around. Whatever happened to your daughter might be about to repeat itself. I'm sorry to remind you of all this, but anything you can tell me . . . anything Anna told you, might be useful.'

She sat there motionless. I watched the wheat outside the window swaying in the breeze. It looked like a desert sand dune, changing shape and staying the same.

'The last time I spoke to her,' she said dreamily, 'she told me she was going to be on television, that she had been assigned a role as one of the dancing troupe in one of those programmes. She was so excited, she thought she had finally made it. It was like the first time she managed to tie her shoelaces – an unbridled pride in what she could do. She wanted me to know that it had worked out, that her career was taking off. Said it like she had proved me wrong.' She spoke with a weariness that suggested she never shared the excitement. 'That was the last time I spoke to her.'

'She didn't say which programme?'

She shrugged. 'She probably did, but I dismissed it all as another of her fantasies. She was good at talking herself up. It's what she did when she had done talking herself down. She had no grip on reality. She lived in a fantasy world.'

That's why she wanted to go on TV, I thought. That's where fantasies came true, where everything was possible. TV has no grip on reality either, which is why it's obsessed with reality, like it's a medicine the industry needs to try to wean itself off the fake, the false, the fantastic. Only instead of reality curing television, reality is infected by TV, it becomes fake and false itself. It changes what's normal. We begin to think something is only truly real if it's been on television. That, I guessed, was why so many wounded girls with low self-esteem like Anna thought that an appearance would make their lives so much better, so much more real.

'Mori took Anna away from me.' She was speaking quietly, almost to herself. 'He was the one that took her away.' She said it as if he had done more than simply drive her to Rome.

'He took away her dream too,' I said. 'He's the reason she never got taken on as a showgirl by the studios.'

'How?'

I didn't want to tell her about the compromising images, about the career the two had forged together. 'I don't know exactly,' I said weakly. 'But it was his fault her dream never came true.'

'And did he kill her?'

I shook my head. 'I don't think so.'

'Why not?'

'No motive. She had made him money in the past, and he probably thought she would in the future.' I shrugged. 'I don't see it.'

'Who, then?'

'It's possible the station's owner had something to do with it. Or someone in his organisation. Your daughter knew about a few financial scams he was running and was threatening to make it all public.'

'Like what?'

I gave her a brief outline of Di Angelo's involvement with the inflated viewing figures and the inflated invoices. She shook her head as I was talking. 'He'll be at home in the Senate.'

'There's no evidence he was involved with Anna's disappearance. He's a major political player. People like that don't get dragged into investigations, or if they do they'll make out they're victims of a political conspiracy. And he's not just a politician, he's still got that TV station behind him. It's like he's holding a nuclear weapon and his enemies have only water pistols. He can aim just where he wants. He's as close as this country comes to an untouchable.'

She looked at me, shaking her head with an aggrieved smile on her face.

'I'm afraid,' I said slowly, 'that it's unlikely you'll ever get a satisfactory answer to what happened to Anna. I keep asking questions, but the answer never seems to get any closer.'

Her face betrayed despair. She looked pained and angry at the same time as she looked up at me. 'Grieving parents always say they never give up. That they'll keep fighting. That's what you always hear them say.' She stared at the table and shook her head. 'I can't keep fighting any more. There's no point. I'm no closer to knowing where my Anna is, or who put her there.'

I didn't say anything. There wasn't anything I could say.

'And sometimes,' her voice was faltering slightly, 'sometimes I think it's my fault. I didn't give her everything in life, I didn't make her life here happy or loving. She left and went to Rome because she hated it here. She hated me too, I think.'

'Why would she hate you?' I asked, trying to reason her out of her melancholy.

'She had good reason.'

'Every daughter argues with her mother. That's normal.'

'This wasn't normal. And it was my fault.'

I kept quiet, expecting her to explain.

She looked up at me, wanting to make eye contact before starting some sort of confession. 'Her childhood wasn't normal.' She shut her eyes wearily as she drew breath. 'There was

164

a lot of poverty in the mountains in the seventies. Not much work and even less charity. I had no family and no income and a daughter to feed. A young woman in those conditions is prey to wolves, and there are plenty of those around these parts.' She looked at me again, briefly, to show that she knew what she was saying, and to check that I knew too. 'You never realise what you've become until hindsight shows you. You don't know until it's too late that a one-off will become a habit, or that you've got a reputation instead of a name.'

She was talking in code, but I thought I understood. And she was using words almost identical to Chiara Biondi to explain how she had slipped into the same profession.

'It started with one married man who propositioned me one day. Said we could keep everything discreet. He would come here after Anna was in bed – she was just a baby – and would leave me elaborate presents. I told him we needed food not flowers, and he started saying he didn't have the time to do the shopping, but that he wanted to look after us, so he would leave us some money.' She shrugged, staring at the table again. 'And before I knew it I was being paid. It seemed like a kindness at first. Someone who cared for us. It was only afterwards that I realised what was going on, when he had stopped coming and the money dried up. I still see him around occasionally, walking arm in arm with his wife as he pushes the grandchildren in a pram.

'We needed the money, and so there were others after that. People began to know who I was and what I did. They knew I was desperate and vice versa. And as she was growing up, Anna realised what was happening. At school one day some children started bullying her and she came home crying, saying her friends had been saying horrible things about me. I tried to reassure her that I was still her mother, that she was my precious daughter, but even at that age she knew that she was the daughter of the village whore.'

Her language had taken on a tone of self-disgust. She blamed herself and her lifestyle for forcing Anna away, and even blamed herself for everything that happened afterwards.

'And what about Anna's father?' I asked.

She shook her head. 'He was just some boy who was here on holiday one summer. That was long before I needed the money, before . . . before all that.'

'Which summer?'

She looked up to the window behind me. 'Well, Anna was born in 1975, that spring, so it must have been the summer of 1974. He left me his address and we thought we would stay in touch, see each other again. But then I wrote to him that autumn, to tell him I was expecting, and all I got back was a letter from his lawyer.'

'What did it say?'

'That his client recognised no responsibilities or obligations and that I wasn't to repeat slanderous allegations about him. After that letter I forgot all about him. I thought I would rather raise a child myself than go through the courts.'

'Why? Surely it might have been a help?'

'The courts can't make a man love his child. If he wanted nothing to do with her, I wanted nothing to do with him.'

'Have you still got that letter?'

'I threw it in the bin.'

I didn't even know myself why I was interested. I was curious,

I suppose, nothing more. I was clutching at straws and hoping that one of the straws might lead to something solid.

'Anna used to say that one day she would track down her father and make him proud of her. Make him realise his mistake in abandoning her. That was her dream.' Her voice was faltering again. 'That was all she wanted: for her father to look at her and love her. Even when she was grown up that was what she longed for. And she really thought it would happen. She didn't realise that maybe that letter said all there was to say: that he wanted nothing to do with her. She still had this innocent idea that she could melt his heart. I think she spent her short life desperately trying to melt men's hearts. That's all she cared about, and she perhaps never realised, until it was too late, how callous they can be.'

'Who was her father?'

'He was called Fausto. Like I said, he was a law student who came here on holiday one summer.'

'Fausto?'

She nodded, and the nod slowly turned into a disdainful shake of her grey head.

'Not Fausto Biondi?'

'How do you know that?'

I stood up quickly. She was watching me from the sofa, confused now.

'What does it matter who her father was? He was never a part of her life.' She was shuffling behind me now as I got up to leave.

'Biondi,' I said, standing in front of her now, 'is the man who hired me. It's his eighteen-year-old daughter, Simona, who's gone missing.'

She looked at me, frowning in incomprehension. 'Biondi?'

'I've got to get back to Rome.' I was in a hurry now, knowing that I'd finally found the link between the two stories. 'Give me your number.'

She found a scrap of paper and a pen and slowly wrote down her number. I looked at it, thanked her and let myself out. I turned the key in the car and sped off towards the capital.

'Any news?' Biondi asked urgently when I announced myself at the intercom.

'Plenty.'

'What?'

'Let me in.'

The gate swung open and I saw the front door of the villa open. Biondi was standing there with his hands on his hips, staring at me like a disappointed sports coach watching failing athletes.

'What's happened?' he barked.

I looked at him and walked into the house. 'Where can we talk?'

He led me through a passageway under the stairs that led to a sunny room overlooking a little garden.

'What's the news? Where's Simona?'

'The news is that she's not your daughter,' I said slowly. 'She's Chiara's child. You and your wife adopted her to stave off a scandal. But she's Chiara's girl.'

Biondi was staring at the seagrass matting of the conservatory floor. He looked confused, his frown so genuine that I wondered what happens to secrets when they're buried that long. Maybe they become secrets even to the person who keeps them, and when they finally come up for air, that person is suddenly surprised by the hidden truth.

'Chiara's daughter,' he said quietly to himself. 'Yes, technically she is.'

'Technically?'

'But she's always been our child.'

'Grandchild.'

He looked up from the floor and fixed his eyes on me. 'What does it matter to you? Daughter, granddaughter – she's missing. She's in danger, abducted by some man we've never met. We want her back. I hired you to find her, not to nose around in our family's past.'

'Never met?'

'What?'

'You said "some man we've never met". She's with someone called Fabrizio Mori.' I passed him the snap of Mori. 'Remember him?'

He stared at the photo as if it were bringing back bad memories. He didn't say anything.

'Tell me how you met him.'

He passed back the photo, looking at me and dropping his head like he had given in. 'I made a mistake in my youth. A moment of madness. I had only been married for a year.' He picked up a petite watering can and started watering the plants on the windowsills. 'I was on holiday in the mountains with a couple of friends. We were in our early twenties, we were carefree. We just wanted some fun.'

'And you found it?'

He put down the watering can, looked at me and then sat down. He motioned to the cane armchair next to him. His head was thrown back and he was looking at the glass ceiling, talking quietly. 'There was a girl there who had a house. Her parents were away, or dead, I can't remember. She had the house to herself and had a few friends staying. We just drank, and played cards and guitars and partied. It was just a few days of fun.'

'This was when? Back in the seventies?'

'Right. Didn't think anything more about it. I got a letter from the girl once saying she was pregnant. I thought it was a wind-up.' He exhaled derisively at his own dishonesty. 'Or maybe I didn't, I don't know. I got a lawyer friend to write a stiff letter and never heard from her again. That was that, as far as I was concerned.'

'Until Mori showed up?'

He looked up at me. 'How do you know all this?'

'You hired me. It's my job.'

He nodded regretfully, as if he would rather have lost Simona than face his dishonest past. 'Mori rolled up here in ninety-one. He asked for an appointment with me in my office. I thought he was just another client, but as he sat there talking I could see my whole life slipping away. Until that moment I had almost forgotten that girl existed. I had never heard of her, never even knew her name. I had my own life here, my own wife and daughter and . . . I didn't want all that disturbed by a complete stranger. Everything I had worked hard for was about to dissolve: respectability, social standing, marital status. Here was this disreputable rogue who knew he had something over me, who knew he could hold me to ransom.'

'What was the ransom?'

'He never called it that. He simply said Anna needed specialist medical care. He came out with some mystery illness and said she could be cured if she had the funds to fly to America. We both knew it was bull, but I went along with it. I wrote him out a large cheque there and then.'

'And he came back for more?'

'Sure. I remember the terror of those months. Every time I went into the office I dreaded the mention of his name. My secretary would say that Fabrizio Mori had made an appointment and I would want to hide under the desk. It wasn't just that I knew I would be a few hundred thousand lire poorer at the end of the day. It was the constant fear that my family life would be ruined, that he could take away from me everything I held dear. And he did it all with a smile and fake charm. There were never any threats or raised voices. He had this veneer of friendliness, and that was worse. He made out he was my friend, doing me a favour. And yet, underneath it all, there was always menace. There was always the perceptible sense that, if I didn't give him what he wanted, he would willingly stop being my friend.'

'How long did it go on for?'

'For months and months. He was coming in every week or so. Taking chunks of my life savings or my inheritance each time. He had a complete hold over me. I didn't realise it at the time, but he was my master. He controlled my destiny. I felt I had to give him whatever he wanted. Every time there was another story: Anna was recovering but needed one more round of treatment. She was stranded in New York and needed the money for a flight home. She needed to buy certain medicines that were available only in London. It was all a charade.' He was shaking his head, smiling ruefully at the mistakes of his youth. 'I knew it was a charade. He knew it was. But we went along with it.'

'What happened in the end?'

'My secretary realised what was going on. She's still with me, bless her. A loyal, loyal employee. She recognised him for what he was and had the courage to confront me. Told me that that man had no business in our office and that whatever power he had over me was imaginary. I'm embarrassed to say I broke down. Told her everything. It was as if a spell was broken.'

'What about Mori?'

'I took away his only hold over me.'

'What do you mean?'

'I decided to stop keeping Anna secret. I told him to bring her round to my office. He started saying she was having chemo in the States but by then the game was over. The next day she was ringing the doorbell to the flat we used to live in. I went down to see her and . . .' He was looking at me with unfocused eyes like he was recalling a distant image. 'I saw her and she was so beautiful and young, she was smiling at me as if the only thing she wanted in the entire world was to be loved. And I took her in my arms and held her. And we both cried a bit. I realised all at once the terrible, terrible mistake I had made. I had shunned her all her life and here she was, desperate just to be held by her own father.'

'You invited Anna inside?'

'I did. We walked in together, arm in arm. She was so happy, she was almost dancing up the drive.'

'And you?'

'I felt relieved in some way. When you've kept a secret for so long, you're almost relieved when it's over. I was shot of Mori who had been draining me of money. And I had met my daughter. It felt like I was finally being honest, like I was reconciled to everything in the past.'

'And you thought your wife would be too?'

'She wasn't there that day. Anna and I were alone and just talked for hours. Talked about her life and mine. About everything, really. She was so young and pretty and she didn't seem to have any recriminations about the fact that I had abandoned her mother. We were curled up together on the sofa, strangers who were immediately intimate.' He was staring out of the window now, remembering it all. 'She left that afternoon and I begged her to come round the next day, which of course she did. From then on she was always here, she spent most of her time here. It was her home.'

'And your wife and daughter, how did they feel about it all?'

He moved the top of his head from side to side. 'Giovanna was . . .' he paused, 'shocked. Shocked and angry. I had betrayed her. So . . . yes, it was a shock. She took a long time to adjust.'

'And your daughter?'

'She and Anna became good friends almost immediately. It was like they had a sibling bond from the start.'

'She didn't feel usurped?'

'What do you mean, "usurped"?' he asked angrily.

'I mean, she was an only daughter, her daddy's special girl. And suddenly, just as she's at a vulnerable age, a rival rolls up for her daddy's love.'

He shook his head. 'They were great friends.'

Biondi looked to me like the sort of solipsist who wouldn't even know if he had upset someone else. He was happy with his lot and wouldn't have understood why some other people weren't.

'What's any of this got to do with Simona's disappearance?'

'I told you before, she's with Mori,' I said impatiently. 'I'm trying to work out who he is. And what he wants with her.'

'And?'

'If he's successfully touched you for money in the past, it's quite possible he sees you as his cash till in the future. He may be wanting a real ransom this time.'

I looked at Biondi. I wondered whether Mori had already contacted him for money to return Simona. It seemed unlikely – I thought it more likely Mori was heading to Di Angelo – but it wasn't impossible.

'Has he been in touch with you?'

Biondi shook his head. 'Why would Mori be interested in Simona?'

I watched him closely again, trying to work out how deep he had buried another of his secrets. His face exuded a sort of arrogance that seemed to eclipse any self-knowledge.

'I think,' I said slowly, 'that Mori's interested in her parent-age.'

'Meaning?'

'Simona's existence proves something. Proves that Mario Di Angelo was making millions out of fiddling viewing figures.'

Biondi put his head backwards, like he thought I was talking rubbish. He looked at me down the length of his thin nose try-ing to figure out what I was saying.

'It might have helped if you'd told me at the outset that you weren't her real parents.'

He shut his eyes, still trying to keep out the past. 'I had

no idea it was of any consequence. She was missing. It didn't seem important who her real parents were.' As he was talking, he seemed to be convincing himself of something. 'We're her parents,' he said weakly.

We sat like that for a minute or two in silence. We could hear the traffic outside and the loud radio of workmen on some scaffolding.

'We did it for the best,' he said in a faraway voice. He sounded softer, and sadder now. 'Poor Chiara. She was only eighteen. It would have been a life sentence to expect her to bring up a young child on her own. She would never have had a life of her own, let alone a family. She made a mistake. We didn't want her to pay for it for ever.' He shook his head. 'Maybe we made a mistake too. But when you've lied once, you have to keep lying, and it gets bigger and larger until there's nothing you can do but let it take on a life of its own. We thought we were doing the best for Simona. Giving her a loving family life instead of leaving her with a young, single mother who barely knew how to lay the table, let alone bring up a daughter. The only mistake we made was loving her too much.'

'And lying to her,' I said.

He turned quickly and stared at me. 'Sometimes loving someone means you have to lie to them. That's the way to protect them.'

'No one needs protection from the truth.'

'Of course they do. Everyone does.'

We slipped back into resentful silence. He was beginning to seem like a pathological liar, someone who couldn't tell the truth to his wife or granddaughter, let alone an investigator. But he said something that made sense in a strange way: he had abandoned one daughter and suddenly had the chance to adopt another. It was as if he could make up for the mistakes of the past rather than repeat them. It was a chance for redemption, he said. To do the right thing. It still seemed like just another deception to me, but I could see how it might have made sense to him somehow. From having been neglectful, he became overprotective.

'Especially because,' he swallowed hard, 'that year Anna went missing. I was just getting to know her and suddenly she was gone. I had a few months with her, only a few months.'

He was full of self-pity. It sounded like he felt more sorry for himself than for Anna Sartori.

'What happened to her?' I asked bluntly.

'To Anna?' He shrugged, shaking his head slowly, his gaze fixed in the distance. 'Mori happened to her. He dragged her round the clubs and society soirées, using her to ensnare unwitting, weak men. Then he blackmailed them the way he had blackmailed me. That's what he did, all he knew how to do. She didn't know what was going on at first. She thought she had to put herself about to get her photograph in those silly magazines. She didn't realise he was getting paid to keep her out of them. She threatened to go public, denounce him for extortion, so he dealt with her.' He rolled his head onto one shoulder and looked at me.

It sounded improbable. Mori had already been denounced for extortion. Biondi probably only wanted to believe he was involved because he held a grudge against the hustler who had taken so much of his money.

'That's why I'm worried for Simona,' he said quickly. 'It's as if history is repeating itself. First Anna and now Simona.'

'I'll find her,' I said, standing up. 'I don't think Mori's a murderer. And I think he needs Simona alive.'

Biondi just nodded, bringing his shoes under his knees and pushing himself out of his chair. We walked to the door in silence.

As he held it open for me, he just nodded like there was nothing more to say.

I caught up with Mori eventually at Tony Vespa's house. I went round there as soon as I left Biondi's place and saw two cars in the drive. One was the same convertible that had been there before, but now there was another car, an old, dented Fiat that looked out of place.

There was no reply to the doorbell. I tried to look through the shutters but they were all lowered. I rang the doorbell once more but nothing happened. The side gate was closed so I scaled it and walked down the path that went down the side of the building. There was another gate at the end of the path and I jumped that too, landing on the terrace in front of two large glass doors. I saw two startled people sitting on the sofa there. The man, Vespa, suddenly stood up and pulled a gun, aiming it from his hip through the glass. I put my hands up and he moved towards me, pulling open the sliding door with one hand as the other kept the pistol on me.

Behind him I could see Simona. She was holding a screwed-up tissue in her two hands. Her eyes were red as if she'd been crying and her hair looked wet and dishevelled.

'You again?' Vespa looked high, like he was getting off on adrenalin. His eyes were excited and he was glowing with weird energy.

'I'm here for the girl.' I nodded the top of my head in Simona's direction.

'She and I are just having a little chat. You're intruding.'

'You normally chat with a firearm?'

'You should see what happened to the last intruder.'

'What are you talking about?' I took a step closer to him, but he raised the pistol and smiled maniacally.

'A man burst in here threatening me and my property. I had to defend myself.'

'Who? Mori?'

'I didn't have time to ask his name. Ask him yourself.'

'Where is he?'

'You can see his feet just there,' he waved his free hand behind him, 'he's having a lie down.'

I made a move to walk past him and stopped. I wanted to see if he was twitchy with the rod, but he let me past. I walked into the room and saw a body lying parallel to the sofa. His limbs were at unnatural angles and his whole chest area was wet with brown blood. I didn't need to look twice to know it was Fabrizio Mori. His long, grey ponytail was splayed out behind him. I looked across at the girl. She was in shock, rocking backwards and for-wards and muttering odd phrases that made no sense.

'Simona,' I said, putting a hand on her shoulder. 'I'm here to take you home.'

She looked at me with scared, wide eyes. She looked like a trapped animal. I knelt down beside her.

'Simona,' I whispered, 'I'm here to take you home.'

Her breathing was rapid and uncontrolled. 'Home?' She looked at me with scorn. 'Back to my parents?'

Mori had clearly told her everything, that she wasn't who

she thought she was. It didn't surprise me. It would have made him appear more honest than her own relatives. It would have persuaded her to stick with him. But now she wasn't only in the throes of an existential crisis, she was also traumatised by having witnessed close up someone getting whacked.

'Simona,' I said, but she was pulling at her hair and moaning.

Vespa's woman, Basia, came in, saw Simona and went and sat next to her. She pulled Simona towards her with an arm round her shoulder. With her other hand she started stroking the girl's hair. They were rocking together now, making a low moaning sound – one traumatised and the other soothing.

I walked over to Vespa, who had his hands on his hips as he looked out across his parched, yellow lawn.

'What happened?' I asked.

'That man barged in here, started threatening me. I had to defend myself.'

'And defend Di Angelo?'

'What do you mean?'

'You were defending his empire. Mori was blackmailing him and you dealt with the threat.'

'I told you. I defended myself from an intruder.'

'You think she'll confirm that?' I flicked my head towards Simona.

'Sure. She'll confirm it. Of course she will.'

'I won't.'

'You weren't here.'

'I know what happened.'

'You think so?'

'I know what happened. Mori checked into the Hotel del Fiume because that was the only way he knew how to get a message to Di Angelo. He knew it was a dive, but he remembered who the owner was from when he used to go there in the nineties. He checked into the hotel with a special guest and sent a message up the chain of command that he had Simona Biondi, the girl who could prove that Di Angelo was running a prostitution ring to skew viewing figures. Di Angelo set you on Mori's case, told you to find him, which is how you and I became friends, right? Eventually Mori got hold of you and you were spooked. This could bring down the whole house of cards – your paymaster's political career could be over. His business empire would be broken up. So you arranged to meet Mori here. You wanted to set up this story about an intruder. He knocked on the door, you invited him in and it was easy. A twitchy finger on the trigger and you packed him off to eternity. Problem solved.'

He stared at me, trying to guess my price. 'What exactly is it you want? Are you selling your silence the same as Mori?'

I held his stare, interested to hear him open negotiations.

'I can give you what you want,' he said. 'Anything you want.'

'Tell me about Anna Sartori.'

He didn't say anything.

'Did you pack her off as well?'

He chuckled quietly to himself as he shook his head. He still seemed intoxicated by what he had done. He was looking at the pistol in his right hand, turning it over so he could feel its weight and see both sides.

'I don't care about what went on,' I said, watching the polished wood of the grip in his hands. 'The inflated invoices, the fake viewers, the call girls and escorts. Not interested. I want to know what happened to Anna Sartori.'

'Yeah, me too. She never showed.'

'How do you mean?'

'Listen, she was a hustler the same as Mori. She was trying to throw mud at a man who likes to keep everything clean. She was sounding off about this and that, the same as that stiff on the carpet.' He flicked the pistol in Mori's direction. 'Di Angelo told me to sort it out, to give her a pay-off. I was just the studio fixer – I sourced girls, sorted problems, smoothed feathers. And there are lots of feathers in TV, believe me. I went round there, he opened his safe and gave me a shoebox of cash.'

'So?'

'I went round to the hotel to wait for the girl.'

'Del Fiume?'

'Right. That was where I tended to do business. It was quiet and out of the way.'

'How well did you know her?'

'Well enough. She had been around the fringes for a while, always pestering me for a role on screen, a chance to step on-stage with the chorus girls. I heard she was about to get taken on until Mori started touting around snaps of her pleasuring men. I sell dreams, but he stole them. That girl was distraught. Di Angelo heard she would have done anything to get back at him or at us. That's why I needed that cash. Truth is, I was a bit apprehensive. I had been ordered to buy her silence, but you can only do that when someone's prepared to sell it. I figured if she was that distraught she might go public whatever we offered her. And then the whole operation would collapse. We would have had the authorities crawling over us like maggots over a corpse.'

'What did you say to her then?'

'She never showed.'

'What do you mean?'

'She never showed up. I waited in that wretched hotel for two hours, having my ear bent by that loser who runs the place. I stood in the foyer all that time, expecting that girl to show up, but it never happened. I phoned Di Angelo who told me to wait some more, so I did. But eventually I gave up, drove round to his and gave him back the money.'

He told the whole story with resentment rather than self-justification. Like he was still annoyed, after almost twenty years, that he had been stood up. I looked at him closely, trying to detect deception, but he seemed, for once, on the level.

'You never saw her? Never touched her?'

He shut his eyes, shaking his head as he smiled. 'I told you. That's not my line. Go talk to that old guy at the hotel. He's still there the last I heard. He'll put you right.'

'And you've no idea what happened to her?'

He shrugged. 'Probably one of her men got jealous. She was the sort of girl who could arouse the passions from what I heard.' He sneered nastily like he was letting his imagination freewheel.

He saw me sizing him up and smiled. 'You still think I'm in the frame?'

'You killed Mori. You're not exactly Padre Pio.'

'Listen,' he said, suddenly serious. 'I've done lots in my life. Haven't always been a giver, I'll admit. I've broken hearts and broken careers. I've made a lot of money out of peddling dreams. I'm no angel, I'll give you that, but that girl's not on my conscience.'

'What about Simona? If she doesn't confirm your version, you're looking at a couple of decades behind bars.'

He nodded with a carefree smile. 'She'll confirm it.'

We both looked over at her. The two women were static now on the sofa, still hugging but motionless. Simona was staring at the wooden flooring as the older woman stroked her hair.

'She'll confirm it,' he said again.

I was surprised by his confidence. His fate was in the hands of an unstable young girl and if she didn't tell it the way he wanted, he was finished.

'You'd better call the authorities,' I said.

He pulled out his phone. I heard him describing the break-in and the threats.

I walked back into the room. I stood in front of the two women and caught Basia's eye.

'She hasn't said a word,' she said.

I put a hand on Simona's shoulder, but she was immobile.

'Simona, you're going to have to answer a few questions for the authorities, then I'm going to take you home.'

She said nothing, but looked up at me. Her eyes were red and her cheeks looked swollen and blotchy. Vespa had finished his call and came in behind me. He sat down beside Simona. He was leaning forward, his elbows resting on his thighs.

'Detective,' he growled, 'give us a couple of minutes.'

I walked outside and stood by the pool. The water was lapping at the smooth marble surround. The area smelt of chlorine and wet soil and cigarette stubs. I heard footsteps behind me and saw Basia walking towards me.

'He's offering her the dream,' she said with derision. Her accent was foreign, but subtle.

I looked back at the two of them sitting on the sofa side by side. Vespa was talking and talking, and Simona was drying her eyes, even laughing slightly as he whispered in her ear. He was talking her out of her shock, persuading and cajoling and she was responding like a newborn to the bottle.

'Which dream?' I asked Basia.

'He's offering her what all those girls want. She's going to get a screen test. A trial in the studio.'

Anna had abased herself for years in the hope of getting that break, and now Simona was going to walk straight in just for toeing the line. I stood there, watching the water for a few minutes as glinting hexagons bounced across the surface, forming and reforming. I called Biondi.

'I've got Simona,' I said. 'She's safe, but in shock. She's seen some stuff.' I told him she would have to make a statement to the police and that I would bring her round after that. He seemed almost grateful.

The authorities turned up and started asking the obvious questions. They took photographs and measurements and asked the same questions again. They wanted to know how Mori had got in, how he had threatened Vespa, what Vespa had been threatened with. Vespa had a reply for everything: he was precise, deferential, regretful. Once they had got the preliminaries out the way, they called for back-up and we were all taken to the Questura for interrogation. We were there for hours. The same questions, the slow tapping of keys by disgruntled office clerks, the forms to sign. The dark night slowly gave way to dawn. When it was all over, Vespa and Simona exchanged kisses on both cheeks like they had a deal.

Simona slumped in the passenger seat of my car and curled

up, pulling her knees up to her chest so that her shoes were on the seat itself. I reached round and put the seat belt over her.

'I'm taking you home.' I put the keys in the ignition.

'I don't want to go back there.'

I let go of the keys, leaving them hanging as I turned round to face her. 'Your parents have been very worried about you.'

'They're not my parents.'

'They've looked after you all your life.'

'I've spent half my life looking after them. I've been a nurse and a waitress.'

I could understand her anger. She had been the perfect daughter only to find out that she wasn't, in reality, the daughter. And that she wasn't perfect either.

'Would you rather I took you to Chiara's house?'

She was staring blankly out of the windscreen. Her face was immobile.

'What did Mori tell you?' I asked.

'He said that Chiara is my mother. That she got pregnant when she was turning tricks.' Her voice raised slightly hysterically, as if incredulous. 'So she got rid of me, gave me to her parents and started her own little lovely family.'

'You're part of that lovely family.'

'I'm not part of any family.'

I twisted the keys and the engine kicked in. 'Me neither,' I said.

We drove in silence. I went slowly, hoping that she might fall asleep or calm down before I took her home.

When we eventually got to the Biondi villa she groaned. I parked outside.

'I'm paid to bring you in,' I said. 'I'm like a bounty hunter and today you're my bounty.'

'This is what you do, is it?'

'This and that. I'm hired by people with problems.'

'And I was your problem?'

'You were. Now I've got another one.'

'Meaning?'

'Come on. Let's go in. You don't have to stay; you're old enough to leave.'

Reluctantly she got out of the car and came with me to the gates.

'It looks like a prison,' she said to herself.

'Biondi,' I said when he came on the line. 'It's Castagnetti. I've got Simona.'

The gate started opening and within seconds the front door was open and Biondi was walking quickly towards us, his wife in his wake.

Simona didn't move towards them. She stood next to me muttering something under her breath. They slowed down as they got closer, seeing her reticence. Their smiles froze and they turned their attention to me.

'Thank you,' Biondi said, shaking my hand with two of his. There seemed to be tears in his eyes. His wife started to hug me and I could smell the familiar scent of booze on her breath. Then they moved on to Simona, hugging her and kissing her as she stood there with all the warmth of a lamp post.

We walked into the villa together. I felt uneasy. The whole place seemed fake now. Before it had felt empty, as if the precious daughter had been snatched away. But now it was simply phoney, an unreal family reunion in which the relatives needed to admit their real relationships. Simona, with all the honesty of an angry adolescent, realised how phoney it all was and was rigid with contempt.

'Darling,' Giovanna said, bringing Simona into the hall, 'you must be famished. What do you want to eat?'

Simona shrugged and didn't reply.

'Let me look at you,' the woman kept fussing. She took Simona's face in her two hands and held her there. 'My darling girl.'

'But I'm not your girl, am I?'

Both Biondi and his wife froze. Biondi tried to fudge the issue. 'No, you're not a girl any more. You're a woman. We should treat you like one.'

'That's not what I mean,' said Simona, her spite rising the more the charade went on. 'I'm not your daughter. You've lied to me all my life. You've never been honest with me.'

Giovanna began to mutter something to herself. She was beating her chest and her head with her palms, the way you see mothers mourning at a child's funeral. And that, perhaps, was what this was. Simona was no longer their daughter and it had finally sunk in. Biondi was trying to say some soothing words, but Simona was just looking at him and shaking her head. She took the well-trodden exit of all angry adolescents and stormed up the stairs to her room. As I watched her disappear, Biondi slumped in a chair by the hall table. He was staring at the floor with a glazed, melancholy look in his eyes.

'What did you tell her?' he asked in a hissed whisper.

'I didn't tell her anything. Mori did.'

'I'll kill that bastard.'

'Too late. Someone's already done it for you.'

He looked up at me briefly, and then went back to staring at the floor. I listened to his heavy breathing as his wife got herself a refill. We listened to the sound of ice clinking in her glass as she poured her poison on top.

We sat in silence for a while. I had grown tired of his self-justifications. I knew that teenagers yearn more for honesty than protection. Throwing off protection is part of the rite of passage of becoming an adult, and poor Simona had discovered quite how much dishonesty there was behind that protection.

'Mind if I go and talk to her?' I asked.

He threw his head over his shoulder as if to say I could go up. As I walked up the wide staircase I could hear loud music coming from behind one of the doors. I knocked but got no answer. As I went in I saw her lying face-down on her bed. I turned down the volume of the music and she rolled over to look at me. As she turned on her side she pulled her knees close to her chin and wrapped her thin arms around them.

'They're not bad people,' I said.

She shook her head, in disbelief or denial. 'They're my grandparents,' she whispered.

'They are, yes.'

She was still shaking her head. 'Even now, they can't admit it. They can't be honest with me.'

'Honesty's a habit. They've got out of it.'

She smiled bitterly. 'Telling me.'

I pulled up a seat and sat near her bed. I felt like a doctor with a patient.

'Let me take you round to see your mother.'

She groaned, screwing up her face at the thought. 'She's even worse than them. My own mother and she never, she never . . .' Her voice gave way and I saw tears falling down her perfect cheeks.

I put a hand on her arm and the contact only seemed to increase the flow of tears. It was like she was letting go of it all. Eventually, she pushed herself up on her bed and growled, staring at me through wet eyes.

'Who are you anyway?'

'I told you. I'm the detective your father—' I stopped myself, 'that your grandfather hired to bring you home.'

'So why are you still here?'

It was a good question. I didn't know myself. I avoided it and gave her one of my own. 'You think honesty's important, don't you?'

'Of course I do. Life's nothing without it. Otherwise, it's just lies and fantasy and make-believe.'

I nodded, giving her time to get self-righteous.

'Can you imagine, never telling me who my real mother was?'

'Or father.'

She looked up at me sharply.

'Did Mori tell you about that as well?'

She shook her head slowly.

'I saw him recently. He's dying. He wants to meet you before he checks out.'

The grunt was one of disdain. She was shaking her head, still trying to come to terms with her confusion.

'Honesty's important, Simona. You're right. Like you said, anything else is just lies. So tell me what happened between Vespa and Mori today. There wasn't any self-defence back there. He killed him in cold blood.'

She was staring ahead like she wanted to avoid the conversation. 'I told the authorities what happened.'

'Told them the truth?'

She didn't say anything.

'Or did you tell them what Vespa told you to in return for a slice of stardom? Isn't that what you want, to get a screen test as one of the showgirls?' Her eyes were glazed over, as if she weren't really listening to me any more. 'I can understand that,' I said. 'You'll be famous, a national icon courted by rich men, envied by your peers. Why not?'

She shrugged as if she didn't want to answer.

'But you'll only get there if you lie about a murder. That's quite a compromise. You see, it's not as easy as saying the truth is important. That we always have to be honest. Everyone makes their own deals with deceit. Everybody has to blur fact and fiction. You can't be too tough on the people you thought were your parents. They did what they did through an excess of love, out of a longing to protect you and nurture you. They lied, but because of love. What's motivating your lie about Mori's murder? Only ambition?'

'I've looked after the woman I thought was my sick mother

for years while her husband stood by and let me.' She exploded. 'They didn't protect or nurture me.'

'It didn't work out the way they expected. But their motive was good. What's yours? Ambition? Vanity?'

She looked away, reluctant to answer.

'Come on, get up.'

'Why?'

'We're going to have an honest chat with your mother. Your real mother.'

She stood up wearily and we walked down the staircase.

'Where are you going?' Biondi asked when we saw us turn the corner. 'Where are you taking her?'

'To meet her mother.'

We walked out of the front door, listening to his weak protests behind us. Simona didn't say anything, but she didn't protest. I walked round to Chiara's place. The street was full of children and prams, people playing football between the cars. We rang the buzzer and the husband buzzed us in.

In the lift Simona was shaking her head. 'I've come here thousands of times over the years, and now it feels like it's the first time.'

'You OK?'

She nodded. She looked tired but stronger somehow, as if the last hour had given her determination and grit. The doors to the lift slid open. Chiara was standing in the doorway of her flat, her face apparently prepared to cry or smile. Simona walked towards her and they hugged. I saw both their torsos bouncing as they cried, holding each other.

'I'm so sorry,' Chiara kept saying. 'I'm so sorry.'

I decided to leave them together. I was just walking back to the lift when I heard a male voice behind me.

'You found her, then?' Chiara's husband was right behind me, looking eager for information.

I nodded. I didn't think it was my place to break family secrets, but I hinted at the surprise speeding its way towards him. 'She's come back rather different.'

He frowned. 'How do you mean?'

'She's not the same person who went missing a few days ago.'

'In what way?' He was curious and concerned at the same time.

'She's different. The same girl, but very different.'

'What did the bastards do to her?'

'Nothing. They haven't done anything to her. It's something that happened years ago.'

'What are you talking about?'

He and Chiara were one of those couples that surprised you: she seemed so beautiful and classy, and he seemed plain and ordinary. You suspected he either had hidden strengths or she had hidden weaknesses. Now her weak point had been revealed, he would have to prove that he really was strong. He was likely to find out that his wife had been the plaything of an elderly, rich businessman and that he was suddenly a step-father to someone he thought was his sister-in-law. I looked at his kind, dull face and wondered how he would deal with it or whether, deep down, he already knew.

'You'd better ask your wife that question,' I said.

He looked at me quizzically as we shook hands. I got into the lift and left them to it.

I had a strange feeling as I drove to the old hotel, a sense that I had overlooked someone I'd thought was a nobody. The hotelier had been useful because he had pointed me in the right direction. He had identified Mori and Simona when she had just gone missing and that was it. I was out of there, I had the scent in my nostrils and was gone.

But now that I was driving back there I began to wonder whether he might know more than he had let on . . . whether he knew something about Anna Sartori's disappearance, even had something to do with it. That's the strange fascination of my job: watching people you think are insignificant suddenly transforming into lead actors. It is as if they step out of the smoke and come to the front, surprising you with their cruelty. Over the years, the job has taught me never to underestimate anyone, never to underestimate the potential horrors that an ordinary person can commit. It has forced me to take everyone seriously, but I still find myself surprised by who steps out of that smoke.

I began to wonder whether the hotelier, after years of seeing young girls cavorting with older men, had suddenly decided it was his turn. Confronted with a vulnerable young girl on her own, he had taken advantage of her and then had done worse. It was just an idea, but it began to solidify as I meandered towards

Ostia. Vespa had said he had arranged to meet Anna there and she didn't show; perhaps the old soak had got to her first.

There was a space outside the foyer but I parked on the other side of the road so that I could watch without being obtrusive. The place still looked dead. No one going in or out. Even the sign for the hotel was lopsided, the top screw having come out of the masonry so that it looked like it was about to fall on passers-by. There was a bin liner on the steps of the place that had been ripped open, and the contents were now falling across the entrance.

I got out of the car and walked up the soiled steps to the revolving doors. The place looked like it hadn't been cleaned for a year or two. There was a newspaper yellowing in the sun, a dirty coffee cup on top of it. I walked up to the front desk and bumped my palm onto the nipple of the bell. It sounded tinny, as if it wouldn't even wake a cat. I hit it again, but got no response.

The steps leading to the corridor and the lift were sticky as I walked up them. As I lifted my soles off the surface, it sounded like parcel tape being unwound. I looked at the same photographs I had seen a few days ago. Pictures of beautiful women smiling at the camera like they were having the time of their life. Some of the snaps were autographed. There were pictures of yachts, of people reclining on deckchairs. Others were in crowded bars: half a dozen faces squeezing into the shot, all smiling and laughing. If you didn't know better, you would have yearned to be alongside them.

The sound of furniture being dragged across a floor drew me away from that fantasy world. I listened again and it had stopped. Then I heard it again, as if someone were shunting a desk across the marble, then pausing for breath, then going again. I walked down the corridor slowly, listening at each door. When I got to where the noise was coming from, I realised what it was: the sound of someone snoring.

The door wasn't locked. I walked in and saw the old receptionist asleep on his bed. He was only in his underpants, one thin sheet half-covering his legs. His huge back was hairy, covered in grey curls that rose and fell as the loud snoring continued. On the floor by his bed I could see, on its side, an empty clear-glass bottle.

I picked it up, filled it with cold water from the bathroom and poured it over his head. It still smelt vaguely of alcohol as it splashed over his large, unshaven face. He woke up quickly, propped himself up on his elbow and screwed up his face to focus on me.

'What the fuck are you doing?' he asked angrily.

'Waking you up.'

He narrowed his eyes. 'You're the private dick who was in here the other day.'

'Very good. Get dressed.'

'I don't take orders from you in my own home.'

'I thought this was a hotel.'

'Yeah, in my own hotel.'

'Got many guests?'

He stood up and walked towards the bathroom, swearing under his breath. I heard him pissing and splashing water on his face. He came back into the room and pulled on his trousers. His hair was matted and he had the incongruous appearance of a tramp with a hotel to himself. He stood up, his large stomach bulging towards me as he put each arm into the sleeves of a dirty shirt. He buttoned it up, and combed his hair briefly so that he now looked like someone who was pretending not to be sleeping rough.

'Tell me, how does this place keep going if you haven't got any guests?'

'We get guests,' he said, not looking at me. 'We get people here occasionally. Enough.'

'Why would they come here?'

He shrugged. 'It's cheap. It's out of the way.'

'I thought hotels weren't supposed to be out of the way. They're not supposed to be off the beaten track.'

He turned round and headed out the door. 'Depends who uses them. The sort of people who come here are the kind that are looking for some place out of the way, if you know what I mean. Married men, married women. This is where people come for a bit of passion.' He looked over his shoulder as he said it and grinned, showing me his brown teeth.

I dragged a finger through the deep grey dust of a picture frame. 'I guess they're more interested in each other than the cleanliness of the place.'

'No one ever complains. They come, they do whatever they do, they pay and they leave. Suits me and it suits them.'

'Sounds very romantic.'

'That's what this place has always been. That's what most hotels are.' He shuffled behind the reception desk, picked up some pieces of paper and bounced them, end on, on the desk.

'What about back in the nineties? What was it then?'

'The nineties?' He smiled and shook his head, the way some people do when they talk about the sixties. 'The nineties? It was party time. This was the place where everyone came. We had a band three nights a week. A queue outside the door that snaked all the way round the block.' He looked up at the ceiling, showing me the grey stubble of his chin. 'That was the heyday of this place. That was when everyone came here. Film stars, politicians, sports stars.'

'Anna Sartori?'

'Who's that?'

'Anna Sartori. One of Di Angelo's wannabes.' I watched his face. He was trying too hard to look confused, frowning too obviously. It was a surprise he didn't scratch his head as well. 'You know who I'm talking about. The girl that went missing.'

'Rings a bell,' he said, looking at me with nasty cunning. 'Yeah, rings a bell,' he said again, apparently enjoying himself.

'What happened when she rolled up here? She was supposed to meet Tony Vespa but he says she never showed.'

'Tony Vespa? That's a name from the past. He still running the girls is he?'

'He had just hired a new one, last I saw.'

'Yeah, that sounds like Tony. He could persuade them to do anything. Haven't seen him for years.'

'The girl.' I tried to bring him back to the subject. 'What happened while she was waiting for him?'

'That's what that other guy asked me.'

'What other guy?'

'The one you were looking for last time you were here. The one with the young girl.'

'Mori?'

He shrugged like he couldn't remember the name. 'He wanted to know about that same girl. Asked what time she had got here, who she was with, all that sort of stuff.'

'And?'

'I never even saw her. Tony Vespa came round here that day, expecting to find her. And ever since then people have been coming round here asking me where she was. As if I knew.' He put his hands together as if praying, rocking the tops of his fingers backwards and forwards.

'You never saw her?'

'Saw her plenty that summer. She was always round here at those parties. But the time you're talking about, the day she went missing, I never saw her. She just didn't show.'

'You didn't see her at all that day?'

He shook his head. 'Vespa had a go at me. He assumed I must have seen her. Or that I hadn't let her in. He hung around for an hour or so and then left. And that was it. I didn't think any more about it until I heard she had gone missing a few days later.'

'You're absolutely sure she didn't show up? You never saw her?'

'I told you,' he leant closer and stared at me, 'she never came in here. Ever since then everyone has been asking me the same question. The police, journalists, Vespa, Mori, you. Everyone thinks she was here but I told you, she never showed.'

His voice was full of anger now, as if I had accused him of something. I looked at his face: it was puffy and creased at the same time, the face of someone who had lived fast and was dying slow. He was trying to appear indignant but lacked the energy to pull it off and he ended up looking pained. I found it hard to think of him as the wronged party. He had been the host of the late-night antics and now that the carnival had moved elsewhere he was still here, trying to party by himself. He was a lonely boozer but at least he was still alive.

There was no point asking the question again. He had answered it twice. He hadn't seen Anna Sartori, that's what he said.

'So what's your theory, then?'

He screwed up his face. 'Eh?'

'What happened to the girl?'

'You're asking the wrong person.'

'Why's that?'

'Because I'm still living under Di Angelo's roof.'

'And you can't dish the dirt on your landlord?'

He shrugged. 'Depends who I dish it to.' He stared at me down the barrel of his swollen nose. 'From what I heard, that girl had been around his operation long enough to know a few secrets. That's all I'm saying.'

'So why would he send Vespa round here if he had already dealt with her?'

'The guy's smart. It persuades everyone that she slipped through his grasp. That's what everyone's always thought, that she ran away before he could get to her. That maybe she was living abroad or in hiding somewhere.'

'What was Vespa like when he was here? Was he just hanging around for appearances?'

'Vespa?' The man laughed. 'He's not the sort to be kept waiting. He was swearing, making phone calls, standing up, sitting down, looking at his watch, looking out of the window. He was expecting her, I'm sure of that. He wasn't there just to have an alibi. He was like a cat on ice.'

I looked around the foyer one last time. It looked forlorn,

like a room that was frozen in time. It reminded me somehow of Anna's bedroom back in the countryside: a place that had been kept exactly as it was, all the incidental positionings lovingly preserved. Only here there wasn't that love, only abandon. It had been left as it was out of laziness. As I was looking around, I began thinking about Anna's mother out in the sticks, about that sad little house by the side of the mountain road.

'And when he came here,' I said, looking at the dishevelled receptionist, 'Mori asked you to pass a message to Di Angelo, right?'

'He asked me to pass a message up the chain of command, sure.'

'What message?'

'He wanted to let them know that he had evidence. He paused. 'That Teleshare was bent in our favour.' It was strange the way he said 'our' like he, too, was part of a glamorous organisation.

'Did he ask for money?'

The man shook his head. 'He wanted to set up a meeting.'

'And you passed on the message?'

'Sure.'

'Who to?'

'To Di Angelo's people.'

'Who exactly?'

'To the accountant who does the books here.'

I nodded at the man at the desk and walked out.

An hour later I was sitting in one of the main squares, enjoying a beer. I had done the job, found the girl and brought her in. I gulped the cool liquid and became conscious of my head swimming with everything that had happened in the past few days, with all the secrets that had come to the surface. But I felt strangely dissatisfied, like I hadn't done my job properly. There was still one, heavy secret that was buried. There was something about the Anna Sartori disappearance that stopped me relaxing and going home. Her fate was part of the same story and I knew I wasn't done.

Through an alley that led from one corner of the square I could hear the sound of an amplified voice. It was an irritating chatter, full of false joviality. I sank the rest of the drink, threw some coins on the table and walked over to where the noise was coming from.

There was another, smaller square that was packed with people. At the far end was a stage made of scaffolding and across the top of it, on a horizontal pole, were half a dozen large black lights looking like beetles on a thread. They were blazing down onto two dozen girls who were twisting their bare shoulders left and right as a man with a mike taped to his cheek strutted around the stage. There was a crowd of about a hundred

standing in front of the stage, applauding and shouting encouragement.

'What's going on?' I asked a woman standing off to the side.

'They're choosing the finalists.'

'For what?'

'For the competition to be the new weathergirl on TV Sogni.'
She didn't take her eyes off the stage as she spoke to me. She
was clapping her hands silently, more in delight than to create
applause. 'That's my daughter there, the one third from the right
in the front row.'

I looked over towards the stage. I could only just see the girls
through a forest of arms that were holding aloft mobile phones.
There, third from the right, was a girl in a sequinned bra and a
very short skirt. She was smiling, putting her head first on one
shoulder then the other.

The woman next to me took out her phone. I heard her
telling someone that they were just about to eliminate another
six girls from the stage. She hung up and put her hands over her
mouth and nose, as if she were praying. The man with the mike
was still walking backwards and forwards, coming out with
mawkish phrases about the beauty of these magnificent girls.

'Please, please,' I heard the mother whispering to herself. She
leant towards me slightly, taking her left hand from over her
mouth. 'She's dreamt of this for years. It's her guiding ambition.
She's even done correspondence courses in meteorology in
order to make the grade. Look at her, poor thing, she looks so
nervous.'

'And you're happy for her to do this?' I asked.

'Happy?' She looked at me now. 'Of course I'm happy. I'll be ecstatic if she makes the final. It's televised tomorrow. She'll be on national TV. Not just a local channel. She'll be famous.'

'Why would you want that?'

She looked at me and just frowned.

The man on stage started announcing the girls who had been eliminated. He left pauses between each name, long pauses that were supposed to increase the dramatic tension but that were so long that any tension was replaced by boredom. As he said each name the eliminated girls would walk along the two lines, hugging each of the other girls as she went. I watched as one recently eliminated waif wrapped her thin, tanned arms around each surviving contestant. She then walked towards the compère, wiping a tear from her eye with the back of her hand.

'Antonella,' he said softly, 'we're very sorry to see you leave.' He passed her a microphone.

'I would just like to say,' she sobbed slightly, 'how proud I am of all the girls here. They are all worthy to win the prize. All of them. They feel like friends already after only one day. Beautiful friends.' She held a hand to her face again, and the compère rescued the microphone as she slipped offstage.

The scene was repeated again and again, as the man left a long, deadly silence before announcing another failed contestant who would then hug everyone and say some dull comments before weeping and being escorted out of the limelight. When the last elimination took place, the woman next to me realised that her daughter had survived the cull and jumped up and down, clapping her hands with her wrists together like some kind of performing seal. Then she turned to me and hugged me.

'She's through, she's through.'

She pulled out her phone again to inform someone about the progress of her talented daughter.

The girls on stage were now hugging again. People in the crowds were hugging each other too. Many were crying. It was a surreal spectacle. The public seemed to be responding to a true tragedy, or real achievement, rather than a daft beauty pageant. I could see one woman in the crowd bashing the palms of her hands onto her forehead as if suffering some terrible grief. Slowly the crowd began to disperse, some moving to the left where the losers were emerging from behind the stage in designer track-suits. Others were moving stage right to congratulate their daughters and girlfriends and sisters on their progress through to the next round.

I moved away a few paces and watched the spectacle: the girls hugging their mothers, and the fathers cutting deals with the producer. After a few minutes the two groups seemed to move together, so that the girls were all hugging and kissing their fathers and the producer, as if to thank them for buying another rung on the showgirl's career ladder.

I saw a large coach entering the square through one of the old arches. It had the insignia of the TV channel written obliquely down the side. Its arrival caused great excitement to the girls, who squealed with delight. There was spontaneous applause as the coach came to a halt in front of the small crowd. The eliminated girls looked on mournfully.

'Where are they off to?' I asked one of the excited parents next to me.

'To prepare for the grand final. It's on TV tomorrow. They're all staying in some secret hotel, there's going to be a big party and VIPs and famous people, and then tomorrow we're all invited to the gala event.'

'VIPs and famous people?' I asked with sarcasm. 'Sounds amazing.'

I knew exactly the kind of party they were going to. Every room would have a casting couch. Just like it did twenty years ago when Anna and Chiara were the young lambs in the lion's den. It amazed me how little had changed. If anything, things had got worse. Back then, a few girls would have done anything to get on TV; now, it seemed, it was more than a few girls. It seemed to be the ambition of all good-looking girls: to smile and flirt and flash their way to the promised land of celebrity. They didn't seem to realise they were no more than steaks served up to portly politicians who controlled the personnel departments of the TV stations. They thought they were entering the world of glamour but were actually descending the steps to degradation. I could understand the naïve teenagers longing to get into that world, but I couldn't understand why their parents colluded in encouraging their ambitions. Why would a mother or father send their daughter into that world? After decades of warnings, they still thought they were helping their loved ones into a different social sphere, into another world where the stardust would be shared round like champagne at a wedding. Even the adults seemed blinded or hypnotised by that world of wobbly cardboard sets, false smiles and fake tans.

I walked away, feeling out of touch with my fellow countrymen and women. I walked to the other side of the square, past outside tables were people were peering over their papers to look at the circus on the other side.

'Coglioni,' I heard one man mutter under his breath. He was

shaking his head disparagingly. I don't know why, but it made me feel better to think that at least one other person felt the same as me.

I only realised I was walking over to Chiara Biondi's flat when I was half-way there. It wasn't a conscious decision but something that seemed to happen by itself, almost as if I was asleep and unable to control my actions. I was approaching the familiar metal gate outside their block of flats when I saw her and Simona walking arm and arm along the pavement.

They stopped in front of me, smiling but saying nothing.

'What is it?' Chiara asked, looking mildly irritated.

'I told Simona's father,' I looked across at the young girl, 'that I would introduce her to him. If she wants.'

'Absolutely not,' Chiara said firmly. Her face looked pained by the expression.

'He was on his death-bed the last time I saw him. If she doesn't see him now, she probably never will.'

Chiara was shaking her head. Having spent years not having her daughter to herself, she didn't want to share her now.

'More secrets?' Simona asked with evident resentment.

'No secrets,' Chiara said quickly. 'I just want to protect you.'

'Protect?' Simona said scornfully. 'Protect seems like a synonym for deceive.'

'Not deceit, not any more,' Chiara said, shooting an angry stare at me. 'I just don't think it's appropriate.'

'Appropriate?' Simona's sarcasm was returning with full force. 'You don't think it's appropriate? You obviously thought this man appropriate when you were my age.'

Chiara closed her eyes as if pleading for patience. 'Do whatever you want,' she said.

'Come on,' Simona said.

'I'll bring her back shortly,' I said. Chiara still had her eyes shut and was nodding now, nodding slowly like she had lost interest in everything.

Simona and I walked in silence towards my car. We both felt bad about leaving Chiara there, but we had our own motives for wanting to see the old man. When we were getting closer to the car, I told Simona what to expect: that he was close to the end and that she shouldn't expect an emotional reunion. He could be cantankerous.

'Probably where you get it from,' I joked.

She looked at me and smiled briefly. 'Who is he?'

'A businessman,' I said vaguely. 'He's called Giorgio Gregori.'

We parked up and walked around the inside of the courtyard to the right door. The old-fashioned brass button gave a loud ring that made the button vibrate as I held it down. Gregori's sister came to the door and looked at us with suspicion.

'He's not even dead yet,' she whispered, 'and you're coming round here hoping for a slice of his estate.'

'Signora,' I said gently, 'this is your niece, Simona Biondi.'

She looked at Simona without offering her hand. She turned to stare at me then back at Simona. 'What is it you want?'

'I want to meet my father,' Simona said.

There was a long pause, as Mariangela Gregori saw herself being replaced in her brother's affections. Perhaps she saw her inheritance shrinking too. She turned round, leaving the door open so we could follow her. I shut it behind me, following the two into the dark corridor outside the old man's room.

'He's very weak,' Mariangela said, frowning anxiously. She opened the door and we saw Gregori sitting up in bed, wheezing in his sleep. His skin was white and the whole room smelt of imminent death: you could almost smell flesh that was rotting in the heat. There was the rancid, sad scent of mortality.

His sister walked up to him and squeezed his hand. He blinked his eyes a couple of times before focusing on her.

'Giorgio,' she said, 'this young woman claims to be your daughter.'

He rolled his head on the pillow and stared at Simona. She held out a hand, but he didn't seem to have the strength to raise his, so Simona ended up waving at him.

'I'm Simona,' she said.

'Yes,' he said softly, 'I see. You're like your mother.'

There was an awkward silence. They didn't seem to know what to say next.

He turned to me. 'This is the girl you were looking for?'

I nodded.

'She OK?' he asked, as if she weren't there.

'She's OK,' I said.

He rolled his head back towards her, looking her up and down. 'You still at school?' he asked.

'No, I'm going to work in television,' she spoke eagerly, like she wanted to impress him.

He grunted with disappointment.

'I've been promised a position in the line-up for one of the TV Sogni shows.'

'Why would you want to do that?'

She seemed surprised that he didn't understand, shaking her head quickly and trying to smile. He turned back to me as if their conversation were finished.

'She's the girl you were looking for?' He sounded confused,

like he didn't remember he had just asked me the same question. He didn't wait for an answer. 'I remember when she went missing. All hell broke loose, eh? There were all those newspaper articles about, about what's he called?' He shut his eyes in frustration that he couldn't remember the name. 'About Di Angelo. They said she had secrets about his businesses.'

'I think you're confusing two different cases. This is Simona Biondi. You're talking about Anna Sartori.'

'That's it. Anna Sartori.' He looked at Simona again, not hearing me. 'Anna Sartori.'

'When did you last see her?' I asked. He was still staring at the young girl, seemingly surprised by how young she looked. He had a strange, ethereal smile on his face, as if he had entered a different time zone, one where a missing girl in her twenties could reappear two decades later as a teenager.

'That man called me.'

'Who? Di Angelo?'

'That's the one. Called me to say she was a loose cannon, to prepare myself for some unpleasant revelations. He said she was going to the hotel, the hotel where he organised those parties. He urged me to contact that young woman I was seeing, Anna's friend. That girl . . .' He lost his thread again, staring, his two fists holding the sheet like they were handlebars.

'Chiara Biondi? You called Chiara Biondi?' I asked.

'So I called her, told her to talk to her friend, to this Anna,' he looked over at Simona. 'I told her Anna was going to go public with everything. That she should persuade her to take his money and go quietly. I said it would ruin her reputation if everything came out. She would be publicly humiliated.'

'Did you tell Chiara that Anna was going to be at the Hotel del Fiume?'

He looked across at me sharply, as if he didn't understand the question. I repeated it, and he gave a faint nod. 'That's where they said she would be. I told Chiara to go round there and sort it out. I always thought something had happened to her, but here she is.'

'This is Simona,' I said slowly. 'This is Chiara's daughter. Your daughter.'

'Eh?'

He was completely confused now about who was sitting at his bedside. And yet he seemed lucid about the distant past. It was as if he couldn't understand where he was now – lying above the trapdoor to eternity – but was able to recall precise details from long ago. I looked at him once more. He was sitting there, still gripping the sheets. His skin was pale but bruised, with soggy veins like converging rivers on his thin arms.

I got up to go, leaving him alone with Simona. The old woman followed me out into the corridor.

'Is this true?' she asked. 'Is that girl really his?'

I just nodded, not wanting to tell her the whole sordid story.

'What does she want?' she asked with suspicion.

'Nothing. Just to see her father once before he dies.'

'That's it?'

'Wouldn't you?'

I peered round the door to look at Simona and Gregori. They were sitting there in silence. It looked like he had fallen asleep again. I walked back in, put a hand on her shoulder and suggested we leave. She stayed where she was, looking at him the way a mother watches a sleeping baby.

When we got up to go, he opened his eyes. Simona took his hand and squeezed it. Then she leant forward and kissed him on the forehead. She was crying as we walked back towards the car.

Chiara was sitting on a bench outside the block of flats when we got there. She stood up immediately when she saw us and Simona walked over to her, crying again now. They hugged and Chiara looked at me, over her daughter's shoulder, with reproach.

'I forgot to ask you one thing,' I said. She nodded, looking mildly irritated. 'When was the last time you saw Anna.'

'Anna?' She paused. 'Anna Sartori?'

'Sure.'

She pulled away from Simona and stood in front of me with her hands on her hips. 'Can't you leave us alone now?'

'One or two more questions and I'll be gone. When did you last see her? Anna Sartori?'

She stared at me with disgust. Then looked down at the pavement, lost in memories. 'We met up in some bar shortly after the station had dropped her. She was in pieces. They had been about to give her what she longed for. She was going to get an on-screen role. And then it was all taken away from her by that man.'

'Mori?'

'Sure. You know what happened. They dropped her like that. Finished.'

'And how long was that before she went missing?'

'A few days.'

'And then Gregori phoned you to tell you to meet her at the Hotel del Fiume? Told you to talk her out of going public?'

'No.' There was a simplicity to her contradiction. No defensiveness, no exaggerated protest.

We looked at each other, trying to gauge something hidden. Simona was watching us, sensing the tension.

'Gregori said he called you, told you to persuade her not to create a scandal.'

'No. No he didn't. I don't think he ever called me. It wasn't,' she said quietly, 'that sort of relationship.'

'He never called you about Anna, tried to persuade you to talk to her?'

'Never.'

I shut my eyes and tried to concentrate. Gregori had seemed surprisingly lucid. He was convincing when recalling the past, like he was almost making a death-bed confession and wanted to express himself clearly. He floated from that clarity into confusion, but I could tell the difference. I knew when he knew what he was talking about, when he didn't have the energy, or probably the motive, to lie.

'We're going inside,' a voice said from far away. 'Please leave us in peace to let us rebuild our lives.'

The voice was very familiar, but with my eyes closed it gave me a start. There was an edge of resentment or self-pity in the voice, a certain huskiness brought on by cigarettes or sadness. I opened my eyes and saw Chiara looking at me, holding out her hand as if she wanted to shake and be done with it. Her voice, I realised, sounded almost exactly like her mother's.

'Good luck,' I said, shaking her hand. 'Look after yourself,' I said to Simona. I watched them walk along the concrete path together, through the cypresses and into the lobby of the building.

'Biondi?' I said into the intercom.

'Yes.'

'It's Castagnetti. It's time to settle up.'

He buzzed me in, holding open the front door as I walked up the familiar gravel drive. I felt like I was coming for my thirty pieces of silver. I knew what I was about to do, but I needed to be paid first.

He led me into his study, a smart room behind the living room. It was lined with books that looked like they had never been opened. They were there as wallpaper rather than literature. He flicked on a green light above his desk, opened a drawer and took out a chequebook.

'So,' he said wearily. 'How much?'

'I've got a few receipts here. Expenses.' I passed over a dozen small slips of white paper. 'Can you do the maths?'

He looked at them with disdain and pulled out a calculator from a drawer. I watched him tapping the numbers in. 'It's quite a bargain.' He started writing, then ripped out the cheque and passed it over. 'A few hundred euros to lose a daughter.'

'Simona wasn't your daughter.'

He stared at me like I was as bad as Mori. 'You took her away from me.'

'She took herself away. The same way you took yourself away

when Anna was born. That's what happens in families. Some people decide to leave. You left. Then Simona left. There's some kind of justice there somewhere.'

'Get out,' he said fiercely, standing up and moving round the side of his desk.

'I'll say goodbye to your wife first.'

'She's sleeping off another session,' he said.

'Where?'

'What do you mean, "where"? She's asleep.'

I turned to walk out of the study, pacing through the living room and toward the wide staircase.

'Where are you going?' he shouted after me.

I took the steps two at a time, not wanting him to reach me before I reached her. I remembered the first floor from when I had first been here, when Chiara and I had looked at young Simona's room. That room had been on the left, so I turned right, and went into each of the rooms: there was a wardrobe the size of a small room, a luxurious bathroom, an empty bedroom. Eventually I found the woman: she was in a large double bed, propped up on pillows and gently snoring. I could hear Biondi's footsteps behind me.

'Signora,' I said loudly.

She raised her head slowly from her shoulders as I said it again, her eyes still closed. She opened them slowly and fixed them on me, staring without moving. Her face looked stony, as if she had woken up to reality and didn't like the look of it.

'I knew you would come,' she said in an ethereal voice.

'Why's that?'

'I knew when I first saw you that you would be coming after me.'

'Why would I do that?'

'Don't be sly.' She smiled slightly, one side of her mouth rising minimally into a tired gesture of amusement.

'What's going on?' Biondi barged in, looking at the two of us. Neither of us spoke. 'What's all this about?'

'Why don't you tell my husband, Mr Castagnetti?' Her voice was strangely serene, as if she were enjoying this last moment of revelation and the power it gave her over her husband.

'Your wife,' I said slowly, staring at her while addressing Biondi, 'was the last person to see your daughter, Anna Sartori, alive. The last person to see her alive and, I'm guessing, the first person to see her dead.'

I turned to look at him to check that he had understood. His wide, disbelieving eyes were fixed on his wife. From having been weak, she suddenly seemed strong and spirited.

'Tell him,' I said to her, bouncing my head towards her husband.

She smiled again, enjoying the endgame. 'All I did was answer the phone. As soon as I picked it up, a man started telling me that that girl was threatening to go public, to blurt out to the whole world what he and Chiara had been up to and why. I didn't know what he was talking about, but as he went on I could work it out. Chiara had been paid to . . .' She couldn't bring herself to say the words. 'She had been his little plaything, and now he wanted her to keep everything quiet. He thought I was Chiara. He was urging her to go and talk to Anna, to persuade her to take Di Angelo's money and run. "Go to the Hotel del Fiume and talk some sense into her," he kept saying, "otherwise your reputation will be ruined. Your name will be all over the papers and everyone will know what profession you're in." I didn't know what he meant at first, but he made it pretty clear. He was talking so much I barely spoke. And as I was listening I could see Chiara's future possibilities, all her hopes and ambitions, melting away.

'That girl,' she sneered as she said it, her top lip tightening over her teeth, 'that girl had come into this happy family and turned it upside down. She had taken away your affections, Fausto, and, with Mori's help, your money. That was all fine. I could live without your money, and I hadn't seen any affection since soon after Chiara was born. That was all right with me. But then that girl started to take away our daughter.' She was getting impassioned now, working herself up into a self-righteous temper. 'At the start of that summer our daughter was a young, innocent girl. She had only just left school. By the end of it she was out until dawn every night, had a drugs habit and was pregnant. That's what that girl had done to this family.' She stared at me with wild eyes. 'I was protecting my daughter. That's all I was doing. I was protecting my daughter.'

'By killing mine?' Biondi was out of control now. His face looked crazy, as if he were capable of anything. 'All this time you've lived here, drinking yourself stupid every day, and all along you knew where my precious little girl was?'

She laughed nastily. 'Don't be melodramatic,' she said. 'You didn't care about her before, so why should you care afterwards?'

'She was my child.' He still had a manic look about him, but his mania seemed about to melt into self-pity. Like a true egotist, he was sorry for himself, rather than the person he was mourning.

'How did you do it?' I asked her.

'What does it matter?'

I repeated the question and pride got the better of her.

'I knew where she was going, so I went to meet her. I waited outside that hotel and when she turned up, I invited her to get in the car. I told her that Chiara was round the corner and needed to talk to her. She wasn't exactly keen, but she got in and as soon as she sat down next to me, I gave her a shot of botulinum toxin. Jabbed it straight into her thigh. You know what that is, Detective? It's a toxin that often grows on sausages and pâté. That's where the word botulism comes from. It's Latin, you see. Latin for sausage.'

There was a nasty superiority to her tone, as if she were enjoying lecturing us about the substance she had used to kill Sartori.

'I had the stuff for my cerebral palsy patients. In minute doses it can paralyse muscles. That's its main medicinal purpose. It can be used for people with uncontrollable blinking or strabismus. Nowadays, though, it's mainly used as a vanity product, as something that helps eradicate lines on ageing ladies. You'll know it by the name Botox. Funny, isn't it, that someone in the glamour industry ended up dead because of Botox?

'Within seconds her pretty face had dropped. Her skin was going dry and pale and her breathing was suddenly uneven. Did I tell you it paralyses the muscles? She was trying to talk, but was only mumbling. Her chin was on her chest as if she were dozing off. Those pretty cheeks had gone a strange grey-blue. I'll never forget that unnatural, stony colour. In less than a minute anyone looking into the car would have thought she was fast asleep.'

'What did you do then?'

'I drove south. Just drove for miles, not knowing what to do.

I'd never planned to hurt her, it was just an instinct, a mother's instinct to protect her own daughter. And suddenly I had this sleeping beauty in the car. I kept driving until I came to a remote bit of coastline near Anzio. It was dusk and there was no one around so I just rolled her out of the car and took her to the cliff edge. I threw her on the ground and rolled her off. I saw her body hit the water and watched it being pulled out to sea. I sat there for an hour or more, watching her float away as the sun sank below the horizon. I still remember the euphoria as I watched her disappear.'

I suddenly saw, behind her drunkard's exterior, her brutal soul. She was relishing the shock she had caused, not just by her actions but by her attitude to them. Her husband was staring at her as if he were seeing her for the first time, her terrible barrenness laid bare.

'I'm going to get dressed. I don't want the Carabinieri to find me like this.' She swung her legs out from under the covers and shuffled towards the bathroom. She shut the door behind her. I walked over towards her bed and looked out of the window. I doubted she was going to run, but I wanted to check that she wasn't climbing out of the bathroom window. I pulled up the bedroom window and leant out. There, to my right and surrounded by wisteria, was the bathroom window, shut.

The deafening crack gave me a shock. The bathroom window was suddenly covered in blood. I raced back inside and saw Biondi standing there frozen, breathing heavily. The door to the bathroom was locked. I gave it a shoulder but it wouldn't budge, so I took a step back and gave it a hard kick with my good foot. The door splintered above the handle and I reached in, found the key and unlocked the door.

She was lying beside the bath, an expanding puddle of dark blood emerging from underneath her head. A stubby, silver pistol was on the floor, under the basin.

I walked out and found Biondi on his hands and knees on the floor. He was hitting his fist against the carpet repetitively. He seemed to be entirely oblivious to my presence.

'I'm sorry,' I said quietly. He didn't look up, but just kept hitting his fist against the floor.

'First my daughter, now my wife,' he was whispering to himself.

I took out my phone and called the Carabinieri. I explained what had happened, who Giovanna Biondi was, and what she had done. I gave them the address and hung up.

From the window I could see the traffic and the Tiber, both flowing slowly as normal. Birds were still shrieking and singing incessantly like nothing had happened. The world was unaware that it should have come to a standstill. From a nearby building I could hear the stoked excitement of an afternoon game show. The host was shouting encouragement and the audience were applauding and laughing. It sounded like a cookery contest, like a race against the clock to do something mundane. I suddenly felt very tired.

No crime had been committed here, so I decided to leave before the authorities arrived with their cameras and questions. I patted Biondi's shoulder and headed out.

The car was hot, and I lowered the window before taking out my phone and finding the number for Anna's mother. I thumbed the numbers in, wondering what I would say to her if she answered. I heard it ringing and pictured her tripping over her cats as she moved towards the phone. I knew I couldn't give her the corpse she both dreaded and yet longed for. But at least she would get some kind of conclusion. It was still ringing, the electronic buzz drilling in my ear. Eventually I hung up, turned the key, and headed back north.

The Dark Heart of Italy

In 1999 Tobias Jones emigrated to Italy, expecting to discover the pastoral bliss described by centuries of foreign visitors. Instead, he discovered a country riven by skulduggery, where crime is scarcely ever met with punishment. This book is his account of a three-year voyage across the Italian peninsula.

'This is the book to take on your Italian holiday.' *Condé Nast Traveller*

'Excellent.' Andrew Marr, *Daily Telegraph*

'Subtle, witty, inventive and intelligent.' *Observer*

ff

Utopian Dreams: In Search of a Good Life

Fed up with cynicism, consumer culture and loneliness, Tobias Jones and his family spend a year living in a variety of alternative communities, from New Age communes to old-fashioned farmyards to Christian detox centres, asking the big questions along the way. Is it possible to be an idealist? Can you be part of a close-knit community and still be yourself? Above all, Jones dares to ask one unfashionable, counter-intuitive question: do communities simply work better when religion, rather than secularism, is at their heart?

'I challenge anyone to read this book without asking whether life might be better lived like this.' Anna Shephard, *The Times*

'Jones probes our modern dissatisfactions with an exemplary intelligence . . . very much a book for our time.' Ian Thomson, *Independent*

'Perceptive, thought-provoking and enormously engaging . . . not only an extremely wise book, but also an important one.' Mick Brown, *Daily Telegraph*

ff

The Salati Case

Fourteen years ago. Silvia Salati's son went missing while waiting for a train. When Silvia dies, the mystery of her son's circumstances becomes an obstacle to disposing of her estate. Her other heirs demand action, and so Castagnetti, a private detective, is commissioned by a notary to change the son's status from 'missing' to 'presumed dead'. But Castagnetti, who lost his parents and his innocence long ago, isn't the sort to content himself with presumption. He likes certainty, and wants justice. Before long he is reopening wounds, exposing family secrets and uncovering a plot as thick as thick and chilling as Italian fog.

'A worthy successor to Michael Dibdin.' *Evening Standard*

'The plot is full of twists and turns . . . But his novel is also, like the best crime fiction, a study of a society and the changes it is experiencing.' *Scotsman*

ff

White Death

Private Investigator Castagnetti is hired by local businessman Pino Bragantini to find out who set fire to his car and why. But what looks like a simple case of mindless vandalism soon turns into something more sinister. After Bragantini receives threatening phone calls his factory is burned down and an employee dies in the blaze. Castagnetti follows the trail laid by an arsonist across the city and discovers that this isn't an isolated incident. It soon becomes clear that the construction business in northern Italy is as cut-throat as it is lucrative. And as Castagnetti is about to find out, it doesn't do to stand in the developer's way.

'A fresh new voice in crime fiction.' *The Times*

'Jones writes with understanding, intelligence and prescience about the country of Berlusconi.' Laura Wilson, *Guardian*